Gallows Bait

Fargo Trent had had enough of being potential gallows bait, so after the bank robbery at Cricket Creek went horribly wrong he figured it was time to ride the straight and narrow trail. It wouldn't be easy but he was determined to make it.

He hadn't counted on the surviving gang members, though. They were convinced he still had $25,000 of the missing loot. Ambushes, kidnappings and cold-blooded murder were all awaiting him.

Trent's only way out was by the gun – the very gun he had sworn to abandon in his quest for peace.

A Land to Die For
Deathwatch Trail
Buckskin Girl
Long Shot
Vigilante Marshal
Five Graves West
The Brazos Legacy
Big Bad River
Reno's Renegades
Red Sunday
Wrong Side of the River
Longhorn Country

Gallows Bait

TYLER HATCH

A Black Horse Western

ROBERT HALE · LONDON

© Tyler Hatch 2006
First published in Great Britain 2006

ISBN-10: 0-7090-8001-8
ISBN-13: 978-0-7090-8001-5

Robert Hale Limited
Clerkenwell House
Clerkenwell Green
London EC1R 0HT

Typeset by Derek Doyle & Associates, Shaw Heath.
Printed and bound in Great Britain by
Antony Rowe Limited, Wiltshire.

CHAPTER 1

BLOOD TRAIL

They shot the horse out from under him just as he dropped over the crest of the last line of hills above the pass. A lucky shot, at extreme range.

But it did the job and the trail-worn grey staggered and went down, whinnying, forelegs folding. Trent just had time to swing a long leg over the saddlehorn and fall away in the opposite direction to the horse. But the posse's marksman had already shot Trent in the right thigh: it had happened yesterday and was still bleeding slightly, sore as hell. He had bound it with a neckerchief and now that leg went from under him, throwing him over to the far side of the slope. He began to roll and slide before he realized what had happened. Then he saw that his wild leap had taken him slightly ahead of the grey, but right in line with it.

He thrust down with hands and boots – no pain in the numbed leg – and hurled himself in a headlong dive downslope. Last thing he needed was to be rolled over by a dying horse whose legs were kicking savagely in its agony.

He sprawled on the downside of the steepening slope, a gravel cascade hitting his shoulders and hat as the grey pursued him, twisting and thrashing, gathering momentum. Twisting to see how close the danger was, he felt his neck click and then he made a desperate move: clawed at some jutting rocks, missed a handhold but slowed his slide and, at the same time, cracked his arm muscles as he pulled, praying the rocks wouldn't come loose. They held and his body jerked a yard off to one side as the grey thundered by, shrilling, wild-eyed, hoofs whipping the air past his face. A knotted foreleg brushed his shoulder, spun him over and once again he was on the slide downhill.

Somehow he blundered past a clump of rocks and a stunted bush, grabbed at it and almost wrenched his arm out of its socket as he jerked to a halt, coughing and spitting. He sat up shakily, watching the horse come to a halt several yards below. Amazingly, it heaved and floundered in an effort to get to its feet.

Forgetting his own battered body, he slapped layers of grit and dust from his beard and slid down on his backside, watching the struggling animal. Still alive and kicking, literally, in its pain, it lashed out blindly at the nearest bush. Its head hung and saliva dribbled, nostrils flaring with each heaving snort. Blood and grit spread across one flank, streaked a leg, splashed onto the ground. Before he even examined the mortal wound he knew he would have to put it out of its misery. It had served him well and he wasn't a man who let any living thing suffer unnecessarily.

He started to draw his sixgun, but stopped. A shot would bring the posse right to him. They would know his general direction but not his exact position. Looked like he would have to use his hunting-knife: he disliked cold steel and the bloody mess that ensued from its use but. . . .

He took time now to look around as he absently stroked the gravel-grazed muzzle, spoke quietly, gentling the dying animal, easing weight off his wounded leg. There was the end of the pass: the posse would be coming through pretty soon. Already there was a yellow haze of dust heralding their fast approach.The other way lay the plains, open country and he would be afoot, with only a half-canteen of water and ammunition running low. That damn sheriff would do his best to see him dead by sundown.

Not if he could help it!

His gaze was shifting about when he saw the great black blot on the plains and recognized it as a herd of grazing bison. He frowned, staring, was nudged by the horse and he gave its ear an affectionate twitch. *Buffalo!* Dumbest critters on the Great Plains. He had put in time as a hide hunter once and with a Sharps Big Fifty, fore-end resting in the fork of a Y-shaped stick set in the ground, had picked off forty-one beasts before the herd had spooked and stampeded. Just looked up casually as he dropped their companions around them one by one, blood gushing, then went back to browsing the short grass.

But, by God, once they got going nothing this side of hell could stop them. . . . He still had a chance! Maybe. . . .

He glanced back through the pass. Hell, that posse was travelling faster than he thought! They'd be here in. . . .

The idea came hurtling into his mind and he reached up, tore his rope, bedroll and war bag off the saddle, spilling them to the ground. Stumbling over the gear in his hurry, he took rifle and scabbard then his canteen and half-filled the bashed-in crown of his hat and set it on the ground. While the panting grey was kept busy trying to lick up as much moisture as possible, he flipped his blanket free, hacked it in two with his knife, cutting his hand slightly, and tied one piece to each stirrup. He avoided meeting the dull, accusing look in the grey's eyes, gave it more water he couldn't afford, then led the limping, staggering animal around the edge of the plain. A glance back through the pass showed the dust cloud had thickened, grown much larger. He could even see the black moving shapes that were the posse men underneath. His heart was hammering, his leg aching and bleeding. His nerves were strung taut as a bowstring.

'Sorry, old pard,' he said into the staggering animal's ear and scooped up a handful of dried burrs, some sticking painfully into his palm and fingers, mixed with coarse gravel. Hesitating only briefly, he lifted the grey's tail and crammed the handful of prickly burrs as far under the stump as he could, leaping aside even as he hated himself for having to do this.

The startled grey shot away like an arrow from a bow, shrilling and snorting, buck-jumping and sun-fishing with its last surges of energy as it hurled itself insanely towards the grazing bison, the blankets flapping crazily from the stirrups. It must have looked like some beast from hell to the buffalo for they were up and away as one, deep-throated bellows drowning the pain-filled cries of the grey as it smashed into the midst of the wheeling beasts and went down. . . .

The ground trembled under his feet as the packed mass of humped and hairy buffalo surged towards this end of the narrow pass, filling it in moments as they jostled and bellowed and crushed their way through towards the approaching posse, hide and hair catching on protruding rocks.

Trent limped back to where he had left his gear, knowing that by now the grey would be dead. He felt bad about it. The posse would scatter to hell and go ahead of that thundering wedge of bison and most likely all of them would manage to get out of the way and survive the stampede. But by then their horses would be spooked, *they* would be spooked, and the pass would be a total mess of churned up ground, as well as piles of dead buffalo that were killed in the crush. There would be no hope of finding any of his tracks. No hope. . . .

Trent shouldered his war bag and rifle, slipping the coiled rope over one shoulder, and limped away into the rugged country fringing the plains. Best thing he could do now was head back into the hills until the posse gave up – *if it ever did!* – then make his way down to one of the remote towns dotting the vast plains. It was risky, but, if he got out of this, he vowed his days of trading lead with the Law would be over.

'Oh, my God!' he exclaimed suddenly, belly knotting and heaving. In his hurry, his panic, *he'd left the saddle-*

bags on the grey! With the bank money still in them!

Clinton Gage watched the band of whooping Indians finishing off their devil's work on the four luckless immigrant wagons. He eased his mount back amongst the brush in the boulders on the slope, tugging his hat down tighter so as to shade his eyes.

Nothing for him to do. The wagons were burning. The bodies lay scattered around and had no doubt been mutilated by the blood-thirsty attackers. He had heard the shooting – scattered, thudding shots – and knew what he would find even before he diverted from his own trail for a look-see.

All he could do now was stay hidden until the Indians cleared this neck of the woods, then try to find his way back to his original trail. Might not be so easy. He wasn't really confident as an outdoor man, at least when he was alone – with a bunch of surveyors or timber-getters it was different. He had plenty of company then and there was always someone fully experienced in wilderness travel and camping. But he was learning, toughening-up too. He hoped!

He watched the Indians, some dragging leather-bound chests behind at the end of rawhide ropes, others waving – or wearing, in one case – women's frocks or bolts of bright-coloured cloth. A trophy raid, he thought, and just then two held up dripping scalps and he spat, hands opening and closing on the stock of the rifle he held across his thighs.

Eyes narrowed, leaning forward in the saddle, Gage watched, straightened, then stood in the stirrups, seeing the Indian band disappear into a canyon leading south. Good, he wanted to go north. He turned his sorrel to start back, sheathing the rifle.

Then his blood ran cold.

Suddenly, silently as death itself, a painted redskin rose out of the rocks to his left and slightly above him. The man had a knife in his hand and gave a wild cry as he leapt at Gage. Even as he dived from the saddle, Gage hoped the others wouldn't hear the war cry but he thought they were too far off for that. Then his body jarred as he struck the ground, jarred again when the Indian landed on top of him, breath gusting from both men.

Gage's nose wrinkled at the rank smell of the man as he fumbled to grab the hand that held the filthy narrow blade the man was trying to plunge into his chest. A knee rammed into his belly and he grunted, upper body rising. The move brought his face within inches of that of the snarling savage and the man spat. Gage's rage erupted as the reeking spittle struck his face. He snapped his head forward with a roar, smashing his forehead across the thin, angular nose. Cartilage snapped and crushed with a crunching sound and the Indian's eyes momentarily crossed. Gage butted him again, broke free and rolled away, groping for his sixgun.

He stopped even before he realized it had fallen from his holster: a shot would be sure to bring back the others to investigate. He reached for his own hunting-knife even as his bloody-faced adversary lunged at him. The redskin's blade caught in the sleeve of his corduroy jacket, jerking his arm to one side, pulling him off balance. The Indian was a better knife-fighter, had the blade torn free of the cloth in a flash and lunged again.

Gage snarled as his teeth bared and choked off the cry of agony as the foul blade drove into the left side of his chest. Gage was already twisting away from the impact of the blade catching his sleeve. It turned his body and this saved him: the blade penetrated, but only a couple of inches, ripping at tendons and muscle, snagging a rib.

Blood spurted with the burning pain and the Indian pinned him to the ground with one knee. Gage fought and thrust and pushed and punched and kneed him away, rolling in the opposite direction. He swung backward with his knife and felt the blade strike resistance. He spun and thrust harder, burying the steel up to the brass hilt, twisting savagely. The Indian writhed, wild-eyed, tongue protruding. Gage kicked away and landed on all fours, then rose, panting, knife in his hand ready to continue. He was shaking like a sapling at the first stroke of the axe. The knife was all bloody, as was the hand that held it and, swaying, lights whirling behind his eyes, Gage wiped a trembling hand over his sweating face and stared down at the unmoving Indian. Tentatively, he worked a boot toe under the man's shoulder and heaved him onto his back.

Gage turned away, sickened. In the struggle, he had gutted the redskin like a trout ready for smoking over a hickory fire. Organs spilled out and Gage saw the body shivering and trembling as nerve-ends died off. The man's glittering black eyes slowly dulled to a frosty brown and the twisted mouth slackened as his head rolled to one side, black blood spilling from one corner. Gage choked, gorge rising.

Retching, he staggered away to the side suddenly aware that his shirt and jacket were already soaked with his own blood. He felt dizzy, dropped his knife and fell to his knees. He groped for the wound, jerking his hand away when he felt the torn flesh and a thick stream of blood pulsing out in hot spurts.

He knew something serious had been severed by that murderous blade.

Gage tore off his neckerchief and managed to wad it over the wound just before passing out. Blood from both bodies soaked into the ground, darkening the soil as it mingled.

The light had a pale, silvery look to it, not brilliant but enough to show the gravel against the dark earth and the ants that were crawling around there.

It was all too close for Gage to see clearly, his vision blurred in any case. Grunting slightly, he managed to pull his head back painfully, lift his face off the ground a little. *What was that creaking, tinkling sound?*

He blinked, stared, not comprehending what he was seeing at first. Shadows moved around a few yards away. He heard the tinkling sound again and after a while figured it was a canteen hitting against a bridle buckle. Gravel crunched under boots. Gage blinked rapidly and the vision cleared some more.

'That's my . . . horse. . . .' he croaked.

The man at the sorrel stepped back in a rapid movement, his hand sweeping down and up, holding a cocked Colt pointed at the startled Gage. The way the man crouched over the gun he knew, even through his weakness and pain, that here was someone who lived

13

with guns and knew how to handle them.

'I've . . . lost . . . mine,' Gage croaked again, staring.

He couldn't make out much in the moonlight, but he saw the man was tall, rangy, bearded, wore a jacket over his shirt and, when he moved, he favoured his right leg. Dropping his gaze, Gage saw the crude bandage wrapped around the right thigh, dark stains on the corduroy trousers.

'Thought you were dead, feller,' Trent said, slightly breathless, still startled by Gage coming back to life. 'All that blood and the way that Injun is. Pretty rough fight, eh?' He limped forward, lowering the hammer spur but not yet holstering the gun. He squatted down about a yard from Gage, grunting as pain hit his thigh. 'Where'd he get you?'

'Chest . . . left . . . side.'

'Hmmmm, nasty. Not much I can do, *amigo*. Stuff a bit more rag in but it's bleeding internally, I'd guess. . . . You ain't gonna make it, I'm afraid.'

Gage stared, breathing hard and heavy, eyes rolling up as Trent stood. This time he holstered the Colt, scratched at his beard. 'I need a horse and you don't, now.'

'You . . . can't leave me . . . here!'

'Sorry, friend. I'll plug the wound but you gotta face up to it. Make your peace with whatever God you believe in – if you believe in any. I can't stick around. Some fellers are looking for me. Like a smoke? Drink of water?'

'Dying man's . . . last wishes, eh! Damn you . . . whoever you . . . are! *Help me!* Don't just steal my horse! He's strong . . . he can carry us both. . . .'

Trent shook his head slowly. 'Told you, friend, it's too late for you. Can't afford to have you slow me down to no purpose.' He swung away, then turned back, taking off his denim jacket. He cut away the remains of Gage's corduroy one, draped his own over the bloody man's shoulders, knelt and wadded one of his own kerchiefs into the hole in his side.

'Could cauterize that wound, if you want. It just might stop the bleedin'. Give you a little more time. Best I can do. Someone might happen along, you never know.'

Gage stared hard. 'Do . . . it, then! Show some . . . humanity, for Chrissakes! Look on it as payment for taking my . . . sorrel, if you . . . like . . . damn you!'

'You sure like to waste your breath, mister.' Trent frowned. *Was he wrong? Was there a chance of this ranny pulling through after all. . . ? Hell, he didn't have time to stick around and find out. But he just might be able to stop the bleeding, give him a little last comfort, some kind of a chance even. . . .*

'You're goin' soft, Trent,' he murmured as he gathered twigs for a fire. He set it in amongst the rocks, after first scooping out a hollow, and placed other rocks around to screen it. Gage, moaning occasionally, holding his bloody hand against the now sodden kerchief, watched closely, feeling weaker by the minute.

'On the dodge, aren't you?'

Trent said nothing, moved a couple of rocks closer to the fire. Gage sucked in a sharp breath, alarmed as Trent took his own hunting-knife and lay the blade in the flames. While it heated he found a green stick, pushed it at Gage's face.

'You'll need to bite on somethin' – save your tongue.'

Gage felt sick. 'I . . . I don't know about . . . this. . . .'

'Suit yourself, *amigo*. But make up your mind *now!* I don't have time to waste.' Trent scanned the darkness quickly. Then he stood and Gage saw he was adamant, the beard jutting from the square jaw impatiently.

Gage nodded. 'OK! Get it done!'

Minutes later he wished he hadn't agreed. Biting almost through the green stick, he choked off some of the scream but not all. Trent ignored him, slapped his hands away when Gage tried to push the glowing steel aside. It sizzled and stank as it seared the lips of the wound. Trent worked at it swiftly after George passed out, burned the ragged flesh away, pressed it in so that it looked more like a large calibre bullet-wound than a knife stab. Might slow the bleeding, though. He had seen the blade the Indian had used, made from a white man's discarded file, patiently ground down on stone, rawhide wrapped around for a handle – ugly, crude and deadly.

Straightening, edgy now at time lost, Trent looked around, listening. Night sounds only. He kicked dirt over the glowing embers, looked again at Gage, and then arranged the man's bedroll, reluctantly leaving the intact blanket covering the unconscious man. He kicked the torn and blood-soaked corduroy jacket under a bush, then took Gage's canteen from the saddle-horn and shook it. It held more than his own so he poured some into his canteen, screwed on the cap and left Gage's where he could reach it.

'Must be loco,' he murmured to himself. 'Man's

16

dyin' with a wound like that an' I waste good water on him.'

But he left it anyway and shortly, after searching for and finding the sorrel that had wandered off, he rode out. The wounded man had drifted into sleep. Or maybe it was the beginning of the long slide down into death.

Trent wheeled the mount away into the darkness. At least *he* had a chance now he was mounted again.

CHAPTER 2

MISTAKEN IDENTITY

'Just look at the son of a bitch! *Sleepin'*, for Chrissakes!'

The posse man who was speaking jumped down from his saddle and stumbled into the camp, kicking at the figure curled up under the blankets.

'Take it easy, Griggs!' snapped the man wearing the frontier moustache and the sheriff's star pinned to his weather-bleached calico shirt. He coughed deeply. 'I know it was your brother got shot in the bank robbery, but we need this one alive!'

'Who says?' snapped Griggs, a solid-looking man of medium height, wide of shoulder and thick of body. He held a sixgun now as the figure stirred and flapped an arm as he tried to throw back the blanket and sit up.

Clinton Gage's eyes were gritty and red and blurred. He saw the vague outlines of the posse men and their mounts, started to speak, but then the pain hit him and he moaned and grabbed at his cauterized side, feeling the plugged neckerchief: did he imagine it or was it not quite so sodden as he remembered last night. . . ? Well, help was at hand now anyway. And the sleep had done him some good.

He struggled to sit up and Griggs, impatient, grabbed him by the shirt collar, pushing away the denim jacket, and sat him up roughly against a rock. Gage's face was like parchment and his eyes filled with involuntary tears.

'Jesus *Christ*!' he gritted, glaring up at Griggs. 'What the hell're you trying to do! I'm wounded, man!'

'You need some sufferin', you murderin' scum!' gritted Griggs and as he moved in again the sheriff snapped, 'Griggs, I warned you! You touch that man again and I'll slap you in manacles and you can *walk* all the way back to Cricket Creek! At the end of a lead, like a cur dog!'

Griggs muttered but subsided, contented himself with glowering at the obviously sick and sorry Gage while the sheriff battled a fit of coughing. The other men still sat their horses, guns pointed at Gage's wound.

'You got him all right, Lasky!' Griggs said, glancing at a rawboned posse man, pointing to the bloody shirt on Gage. 'Too bad you didn't nail him dead centre.'

'Hell, he was nigh on four hundred yards and still goin' away as it was!' Lasky drawled. There was pride there.

'You did good,' the sheriff wheezed, breathless, wiping his mouth. Lasky nodded stiffly, accepting his due.

Gage ran his hot gaze around the posse and felt the

19

first twinges of apprehension. Maybe there wasn't as much hope for salvation here as he had first thought. Something was wrong!

'Sheriff . . . You're from Cricket Creek?'

Griggs threw the lawman a savage look. 'C'mon, Dub! He's gonna be smart-mouth! Lemme at him for a five minutes, just five! I'll make him tell where the rest of his gang is!'

The lawman lifted a gnarled hand without looking at Griggs. He was studying Gage. 'Sheriff Dub Bracemore from Cricket Creek, mister. And your name'd be "Trent", right?'

'Wrong!' Gage almost shouted, wincing again and grabbing once more at his side. He fought for breath. 'I . . . I'm Clinton Gage . . . I work for. . . .'

Griggs couldn't control himself any longer. He lunged forward and slapped Gage across the face, spilling him onto his side. Griggs looked challengingly at Bracemore but the sheriff didn't say anything, though he did lift a halting hand as Griggs started to move in again. The blocky man stopped reluctantly.

'Mister, your name is *Trent*!' the sheriff said tightly, fighting another coughing bout. 'This here posse under me has been trailin' you for three days – four if you count this mornin' – after you and your gang robbed our bank and killed a teller and a bystander durin' your escape and now we've caught up with you and by Godfrey I'm in no mood for any stupid shenanigans! You been shot, put afoot and you're caught. . . . I'm takin' you back to Cricket Creek and you're gonna get a fair trial, but I can tell you now, feller, you can look forward to a hemp necktie before the week's out!'

Bracemore spat to the side angrily, chest heaving as he glowered at the stunned Gage. '*Now*, you gonna co-operate? Or do I let Griggs have his way with you? His brother was the bank teller, by the by. . . .' The sheriff coughed hard.

Gage felt sick. His head was thundering. His wound hurt, but the bleeding had eased. 'Sheriff . . . please . . . just hear me for a minute. All right?'

Griggs snarled, fists bunched, and after a few moments Sheriff Bracemore nodded. The other posse men all showed their contempt and hate for Gage. Two started going through the few things surrounding him: canteen, the blanket, the stained denim jacket. No one noticed the old corduroy jacket hidden by a bush.

'No sign of the money, sheriff,' a man called and Gage moved uncomfortably. 'No saddlebags, that I can find.'

'That's queer. He had to be carryin' money. . . .'

'Sheriff, I can prove who I am – Clinton Gage, as I said.' Gage flinched as Griggs just managed to stop himself hitting him. 'I work for a company called Trans-Continent. We're kind of a help agency for people who want to develop the West . . . It's a new concept, called "consultancy". . . .'

'What's this goddamn hogwash, Dub. . . ?'

Bracemore waved Griggs to silence. 'I've heard of that thing. Run by a bunch of Eastern millionaires, ex-railroad men or from construction companies exploited the East, now they got their eyes on the West.' He looked steadily at Gage, two bright patches on his withered cheeks. 'You're one of them know-all bastards who travels around, arrangin' surveys, buyin' land after beatin' down some poor sonuver to bedrock bucks. *Then* you supply materials, at *your* prices!'

Gage managed a fleeting smile. 'Not . . . exactly. And I wish to stress I am of legitimate birth, sheriff. You've been listening to hearsay: Trans-Continent operates honestly. The men who back the agency have a genuine desire to see the West open up for all comers, from all walks of life, and their aim is to bring as many comforts as possible to them.'

Griggs belted Gage across the mouth and blood flowed, together with a broken tooth. The sheriff waved to two younger posse men and they swiftly dismounted and hauled Griggs back. The wounded man was sprawled on the crumpled blanket now, fresh blood on his side, his consciousness wavering.

Gage, palefaced, sweating, was allowed to get his breath and, inching away from Griggs, he looked again at the sheriff. 'I consider my work is worthwhile, despite what you think. I scout for the best locations for railroad routes, dam sites, even future towns. We make recommendations to the Federal Lands Department and, when they approve, arrange for supply of surveyors, building materials and workers at better rates than most companies could hope to get by themselves. Mutual benefit all round.'

'And those fat bastards in Boston and Philadelphia or wherever they have their holes grow fatter and richer without liftin' a finger!' growled Griggs. 'What you really do is check out banks that're worth robbin'! *Or maybe a payroll run, huh?* That's your real goddamn job!'

'I am employed by Trans-Continent, damn you! I've been scouting this general area for some time now:

there are plans for railroads coming in from the south and the east to meet up at a location I was on my way to recommend, where an entirely new town will be built with cattle-holding facilities. Something like what Joe McCoy did for Abilene only adapted to local conditions. . . .'

'Enough of this hogwash!' Griggs shouted. 'You sure have the gift of the gab, mister! He's figured a story but he ain't what he claims, Dub, you *know* he ain't!' He turned on Gage. 'You're name's Trent and you robbed our bank and killed my brother, you lyin' snake!'

Bracemore signed wearily to the two young posse men and they grabbed Griggs, disarmed him and sat him down roughly against a rock. He glared his hate at both the sheriff and Gage as the latter said, 'I have papers in my saddlebags that . . . Oh!'

He stopped. He suddenly realized Trent had taken all his things with him when he took his sorrel. Gage sounded and looked almost pitiful as he tried to explain what had happened to him. He pointed at the body of the Indian that had been dragged off a short distance and worked on by night animals, crawling with insects now. 'There's your proof. He's the man who knifed me!'

Desperately, he removed the wadded rag from his wound. The sheriff and the others examined the puckered wound.

'By hell, that looks like a bullet wound to me!' Griggs said.

The others agreed, Lasky, the marksman saying, 'Could be where I winged him the day before I shot his hoss, Dub. Ain't no knife wound, that's for sure.'

'What d'you have to say about that, mister?'

'Look at the blade on that Indian's knife! It's more like a spear point than a knife. Trent cauterized my wound, too, changed its looks, I guess. . . . Why can't you believe me?'

Griggs held up the crumpled and stained denim jacket. 'This is the jacket Trent was wearin' when he cleared town with his gang! He was the only one wearin' a jacket an' he tripped in a puddle in his hurry and *there's* the damn mud stain, see? It's *your* jacket, you son of a bitch!'

'No! Mine was ruined in the knife fight!' Gage looked around wildly. 'It must be somewhere around here. . . . Trent left me that jacket you're holding before he rode off on my horse! With all my papers in the saddlebags, and. . . .'

There was a cursory search but no one saw the damaged corduroy jacket beneath the bush where Trent had thrown it. Not that anyone tried hard: they *knew* they had 'Trent'. He was their man, all right.

'He took my horse! Cauterized my wound and left me his jacket, I tell you!' Gage's voice cracked with his intensity. All this tension and harsh treatment was getting to him now. Sweat drenched him and his breath came in panting gasps, the world spun as he fought to make them understand.

'Why would you think we'd believe a murderin' scum like Trent'd do any of them things?' Dub Bracemore asked. The man looked desperately tired, but still dangerous. His eyes were very bright and he spat some phlegm. 'We *know* Lasky here shot your hoss from under you yesterday. He winged you before that and you had to try to stop the bleedin' and passed out likely when you cauterized the wound . . . Slept too heavy, friend! Now you're headed for the deepest sleep of all. Get the manacles on the sonuver and put him on one of the pack hosses!Folk back in town are just waitin' to get a close-up look at one of the bastards who robbed the bank of their money . . . and I need my medicine for this goddamned cough before I bring up a lung!' He demonstrated by going into a wracking bout.

Gage said wearily. 'Search all you want. There's no money here!'

'We know your gang separated soon as you cleared town. You either buried your share before you stampeded them buffalo or your pards are holdin' it for you.'

'My name is not "Trent"! You can't pin this crime on me! I'm innocent! A telegraph to Trans-Continent in St Louis will establish my identity and. . . .'

Griggs managed to kick Gage's legs from under him and massage his ribs with a size twelve riding-boot before he was hauled off roughly. He turned a tightly smiling face to the lawman. 'Seems we've heard that before, Dub!'

'Get him ready,' snapped Bracemore. 'I'm a-wearyin' of this.' He turned to a rangy man with thick wrists and a cast in one eye. 'Reckon you can throw up a gallows in a few days, Rusty?'

'You gimme a County contract and it'll be done, Dub! Fact, I'll build you a gallows that'll stay there permanent, come hell or high water!'

'Sounds like a good idea. Make an example outta this feller, warn off others who might have notions of robbin' our bank,' agreed the ailing sheriff.

Gage's legs wouldn't support him and he had to be carried and lifted onto the back of one of the patient pack animals. He felt dizzy and sick.

Somewhere, he thought in a burst of futile bitterness as they roped him in place, *somwhere, I hope you're suffering, Trent! Dying of thirst or hunger or* . . . or the sorrel has collapsed and pinned you by the legs in the alkali and it's a hundred and twenty degrees in the shade! Oh, yes, Trent, you son of a bitch! I hope you're suffering like hell!

CHAPTER 3

RENDEZVOUS

There was no one waiting at the first rendezvous.

It didn't surprise Trent. The gang had scattered far and wide and Bracemore would have put out more than one posse. Like him, the gang members were probably still trying to dodge the pursuers.

Just to be sure, he scouted around, finding the sorrel an obedient animal having no hesitation in plunging into screening brush or negotiating eroded draws, even obvious cutbanks. Seemed to him it was an animal used to rough country. Which surprised him some, for he hadn't picked that wounded ranny as the type who would spend a lot of time riding through the wilderness. There was a lot of tenderfoot in that feller.

Then again, he had seemed muscular enough when he had cauterized his wound: he must have done a heap of riding or manual work, just looked a mite on the soft side.

Anyway, he was most likely dead by now. Trent felt a

mild twinge of conscience. Maybe he could have, should have, done more for him, but hell, a man had to take care of himself. He'd made his passing a little more comfortable anyway and that was about as much as any man had a right to expect these days. Specially out in this Godforsaken country.

He put all thoughts of Gage from him and concentrated on the rendezvous area, making sure it wasn't staked out by some eager posse members who might have already jumped any of the bunch who had arrived early.

There was no one waiting and he swore softly, patted the sorrel's sweating neck and headed for the creek. He would top up his canteen, wished he hadn't left the other one with the wounded man because he was heading into mighty dry country now between here and the next rendezvous.

But he was underway in an hour, belly empty, jaws sore from chewing on some fluff-covered jerky he found in the bottom of one saddlebag. There were papers in there and he glanced at them as he rode slowly up a twisting trail over a broken-backed mountain. The wounded man was named Clinton Gage. He couldn't really fathom what he did for a living, but it had something to do with a company called Trans-Continent. Trent thought he had heard of it but wasn't really interested. Fact was, his conscience still bothered him some for abandoning Gage that way. Strange but lately he had found himself thinking more about his deeds and whether they were right or wrong. Hell, most were *wrong* in the eyes of the Law but that didn't trouble him so much. He was still a Johnny Reb at heart and

Tag Benedict's bunch, which included him, operated mostly in Yankee territory.

The war had ended six years ago and it had felt good for a long time continuing to roust the Yankees. But a couple of years ago it had mostly lost its appeal. Now he was, what? Pushing twenty-six or seven and didn't know where the hell he was going. Or even how long he could stay alive. Tag's jobs were getting more and more risky:the man was too damn reckless, drank too much, pickled his brain. That last deal at Cricket Creek had been mighty chancey. He'd played it close to his chest and gave out only the barest details. Pete someone, the man who had spied out the ground for them, said that because of the payroll for the mine being kept in the bank's safe overnight, there would be armed men guarding it, special deputies hired by Dub Bracemore, the local sheriff.

'Armed deputies never have bothered us,' Benedict had said, taking another swig from his bottle, wiping his thin-lipped mouth on the back of a hairy wrist.

'There'll be four, Tag,' warned the informant, a nervous townsman who looked as if he wanted to share the bottle with Benedict. ' 'Specially picked for their meanness.'

Benedict snorted and spat. 'They dunno what mean is till we set our sights on a payroll that size!'

He was an average-sized man, Tag Benedict, but looked and was tough. He jerked his head at Chuck Keel. 'Take Pete and pay him, Chuck, then see him safely on his way.'

Trent had tensed then, catching something in Tag's tone and the look he exchanged with Keel, a mean sonuver. He stood and said, 'I'll see Pete off, Tag.'

Benedict lifted his eyes under their heavy black brows. 'Siddown, Trent. Chuck's got the pay-off money for Pete. He knows what to do.'

Trent was uneasy but he sat down. Chuck and the informer quit the camp and went away into the darkness. It was some time before Keel came back and when he did, he took his knife from its sheath and began to polish the blade with a handful of sand.

His fingers were red and sticky. . . .

That was when Trent decided this would probably be his last job with the gang. Get his share, cut and run.

They had been a wild-ass bunch to start with, fanatics, almost, in their hatred for Yankees . . . himself, Tag, Big Tom, Chuck Keel, Cherokee, Old Sampson. Now that hatred, in him at least, was blunted and he knew it was time to quit and start living a regular life – whatever that was. As long as it didn't include lawmen hounding him, or having to sneak into towns to check the post office for wanted dodgers, sleeping with a gun in his hand under the blankets, and a dozen other things that tore at a man's nerves.

He definitely decided that Cricket Creek would be the last job: there would be a goodly amount of money for his share and he would use it to ride south, look for somewhere he could settle, maybe find a place of his own, working for someone else if it seemed like the best idea.

But this would be his last job, for sure. *Tag didn't need to know. Fact, it would be better if he didn't know. Yet.*

He knew there would be trouble with Benedict and the others but he was prepared for that, too. Only thing

30

he wasn't prepared for was how badly things had gone wrong.

Just like Pete had warned, there were armed deputies patrolling all round the bank, three instead of four, but three was enough. They didn't want any gunshots, which meant stalking the deputies and clubbing them unconscious. He thought at least one had fallen to Chuck Keel's knife.

Right then Fargo Trent had been going to walk away. He should have but Tag came out of the shadows, his footsteps muffled by the light rain that was falling on the leaves of the bushes behind the bank building.

'All clear,' called Benedict softly. 'Get that rear door open, Trent. Won't be long till daylight.'

That was another thing: Pete had said there was only a draw-bolt with a padlock on the door. There was but because of the payroll, no doubt, they had taken the precaution of drilling a hole through the heavy door and fitting an extra chain and padlock. It took a hell of a long time to file through a link of the chain and by then the rain had stopped and there was grey in the east and shadows began to take on detailed forms: bushes, crouching men, the getaway mounts and townsmen already moving about on their way to work, stores opening, the saloon swampers throwing their slops into back alleys not far from the bank.

Using a file and axle grease scooped from the hubs of a nearby parked teamless buckboard, Trent had managed to get the chain cut free, more or less silently. There must have been a padlock on the inside, too, for something dropped with a thud he felt half the town must have heard when the chain parted.

But they were inside seconds after the chain was pulled free and the draw-bolt prised off by Big Tom. Somehow, without Pete or anyone else knowing about it, a barred iron door had been set across the normal door of the room where the huge safe was kept. It, too, had a chain and padlock and that was too much for Tag Benedict.

'Hell with this! It's gonna take all day! We got dynamite for the safe, well, looks like we're gonna have *two* explosions instead of one.' He motioned up Cherokee and Sampson and pointed at the barred door. 'Blow that son of a bitch open! Then don't waste no time in gettin' to the safe!'

'Judas, Tag!' wheezed Sampson, oldest member of the gang. 'We're gonna have to work fast! The first bang'll bring Bracemore in his nightshirt and a Greener in each hand! Then we'll still have the safe to blow!'

'Well, what the hell you standin' here for?' growled Benedict. 'Get the thing done!'

He dropped a hand to his gun-butt and Sampson nodded. Cherokee was already taking sticks of dynamite from the gunny-sack he carried. They used a short fuse and Tom found a mattress on a small bed in the bank's sick-room for staff members and all the bankets, pillows and towels. They had originally planned to use these to muffle the safe blast but they worked just as well on the barred door.

It was like a snowstorm in the room after the dull, ear-thumping thud of the explosion. Feathers from the pillows and mattress filled the air. Someone sneezed, others waved hats around to clear a way to the now bent and sagging barred door. It was still dull inside the building and Trent held a lantern while Cherokee and Sampson packed four sticks of dynamite along the edges of the heavy, green-painted safe door, sticking them into the groove with beeswax.

'They'll think a damn earthquake has hit town!' Trent said but Cherokee shrugged, dark eyes flicking briefly to Trent, then back to the job in hand.

'Tag said use six but four ought to do it.'

'Madman! It'll blow the rear wall out!'

'Fuse's lit!' yelled Sampson and they ran into the dim foyer of the bank, crouching behind the heavy counters.

It went with a thunder that blew out all the glass in the windows and the street doors, sent papers swirling and floating all through the passage and in the manager's office. Choking nitro fumes set them all coughing and then Benedict and Keel thrust up to the safe, scooped up the specially marked payroll bags and one leather satchel. Tag shouldered through, snatched two bags and the satchel from Cherokee and Sampson.

'Let's go!' he bawled and Cherokee, now looking out the shattered front doors, called in his clipped, growling voice, 'They comin' already! Sheriff's all dressed – guns, too. Look like they been ready an' waitin' for us. . . .'

'We're ready, too!' snapped Benedict, crouching a little to glance up the street, arms cradling his thick bags and the small satchel. It had some kind of seal on the flap. 'C'mon!'

Then a citizen, later identified as one Willis Griggs, teller, on his way to open up the bank early for the manager to release the mine payroll, appeared dragging a sixgun awkwardly from his belt. Without hesitation, Tag shot him through the shattered glass panel of the street door, two deadly bullets taking the man in the chest. The sheriff opened fire, the charge from his Greener blowing most of the damaged door away, leaving the front of the bank wide open. By then the robbers were running out the back and when they got to their getaway mounts, they saw another townsman at the parked buckboard with a horse ready to hitch up.

'Hey, what the hell you fellers up to?' he bawled.

These were the last words he spoke. Keel and Cherokee fired together, the townsman's body jerking and twisting as he went down. The shots startled Trent's horse and it broke free from his grip as he was about to mount. He ran after it, slipped, cannoned into Tag and fell into a puddle, his shirt and jacket dripping mud as he angrily got to his feet. He caught the trailing reins and turned as Benedict got groggily to his feet, bags and satchel, scattered around the ground. Trent snatched up a double-sewn canvas pouch and the satchel, rammed them into his saddlebags. Benedict shouted something at him. Then more armed men were running down the street, shooting wildly as Trent leapt into the saddle. Half the damn town was awake by now, all armed and shooting. Bullets whined off the brick walls of the bank, splintered clapboards on the building next door, tore leaves and twigs from the bushes as the gang wheeled and rode away. Benedict was still shouting but the shooting drowned his words.

'Mounts! Mounts!' Sheriff Bracemore bellowed.

Two men were leading a bunch of already saddled

mounts from the back door of the livery. Trent glimpsed them and swore: looked like they had been expected, all right. Maybe, as Tag and Keel had suspected, Pete had been working both sides of the street, taking pay from the gang as well as the sheriff. . . . Too late now. All they could do was ride like hell and try to meet up again at the pre-arranged rendezvous.

He hoped Tag Benedict had the rest of the money safely secured after all this trouble. He reached the end of town with more bullets whistling overhead and veered sharp left, going south. Tag and the rest of the gang scattered and by that time, the posse was coming, at least a dozen men, more still mounting-up in the streets. They would scatter too, a few men going after each gang member. *What a lousy deal! They'd be lucky to get out of this one alive!*

It had been a close call all right, after that posse sharp-shooter winged Trent in the right thigh, then shot the damn horse from under him the very next day. Luckily the buffalo stampede had slowed them down. He had been riding Gage's stolen sorrel for three days now without sighting a dust cloud hanging in the air along his back trail so he figured it was safe to head for the first rendezvous.

And, of course, there was no one waiting. He was surprised. And relieved too, in one way: he wasn't looking forward to telling Tag Benedict he had left the cash bag and satchel on his horse when he had sent the dying grey into the buffalo herd. He had been close to panic, what with the bullet in his leg, taking such desperate measures. But he went to the second rendezvous and it too was empty, though there was sign that someone had been there recently. Not the whole bunch, but at least one other rider. *Tag?* he wondered. Well, that left only the third and last meeting place where they had arranged to re-group. He almost passed it up but decided he might as well check.

It was in a small canyon with sandstone walls. He rode in warily, sniffed the campfire smoke and relaxed a little. On the approach he had studied the walls closely but had not seen any guards. There should've been one man at least on lookout, holding him in the sights of his rifle, making sure the rider was who he seemed. He hoped they recognized him, for he was forking a sorrel now instead of his usual grey and he had left his denim jacket with Gage. *Damn fool move, that! Knew the man was dying and gave him his jacket to keep him warm! Christ, he'd better give up the owlhoot trail and go straight! He was going soft in the head!*

He rode through a twisting cleft carefully, sixgun in hand now, remembering how the hidden passage doubled back on itself at a point where a boulder jutted out. It was an awkward turn and the best place for an ambush if lawmen were trying to find a way in.

But *he* wasn't expecting to be bushwhacked.

So when the bullet whined off the jutting boulder, striking sparks, he jerked sideways in the saddle, shoulder hitting the wall the turn was so tight. He reacted instinctively, the sixgun coming up and blasting two swift shots at the spurt of smoke showing on the narrow ledge to his right and several feet above.

It caught the ambusher off guard, not expecting such a lightning reaction. The bullets whined and one at least ricocheted down onto the ledge. He triggered the rifle in a wild shot and Trent's sixgun blazed before its echoes died. The man cried out, jerked and rolled away, revealing his patched brown shirt. Trent saw it was Cherokee.

He didn't waste words: the halfbreed was a quiet man but he was mean and enjoyed killing. Holding his frightened sorrel by one taut rein, Trent stood in the stirrups as the breed groped for the rifle and shot with a steady hand.

The body tumbled down into the narrow passage and Trent, still mounted, looked around warily. No sign of any more guns. He could see round the last bend into the small canyon itself now. No horses tethered under the big shady rock overhang. A small campfire burning – Cherokee would have set that so he could smell the smoke and ride in unsuspectingly.

He rode right up to where Cherokee lay, blood on his shirt-front and at a corner of his mouth, dark face a kind of yellowish-grey. Trent kept the sixgun pointing down at him.

'Tag leave you behind to take care of me and whoever else showed up so he wouldn't have to share the loot? Kill me, take what I was carryin'? Missed the other places on purpose, figurin' it'd bring me ridin' in here hell-for-leather, reckless, careless.'

The breed's nostrils were pinched with his laboured breathing and his dark eyes glittered malevolently. He hadn't gotten along well with Trent, nor any other gang member for that matter.

Trent bared his teeth in a tight, humourless grin. 'You reckon he would've given you *your* share when you finally caught up with him again, Cherokee?'

The breed made a kind of growling sound.

'You're a damn fool, Cherokee. Tag and Keel don't aim to share that money nohow! I seen it comin', only rode up here to explain that I was quittin'.'

'Tag expect that . . . my horse lame . . . tell me take yours . . . and bring the saddlebags.'

'Then he was in for a surprise . . . never mind why.'

'I happy to kill you, Trent! Never liked you!' He coughed and bright red blood ran over his chin. 'Never did.'

'Mutual, Cherokee. You're lungshot, man. Dyin'.'

'So . . . it's my time to . . . die! Who . . . cares!' His voice had a bubbly sound now and he choked on a mouthful of his blood. His hate was a tangible thing, not just for Trent, but for the whole damn world that he figured had treated him like dirt all his life. The only reason he was clinging to these last few moments was to express that hate as well as he could. 'I got no one . . . don't need . . . no . . . one.'

Trent nodded. 'Want to lie there and die slow? Or . . .' He lifted the gun as if he would shoot the breed.

The breed stared up, blood flowing darkly over his chin now, curled a glistening red lip into a snarl. Trent waited, finally turned towards his horse, ramming the Colt into his holster.

He was ready to leave when Cherokee grated, 'Bullet!'

Fargo Trent nodded, drew his gun again and stared down into those hate-filled burning eyes for a moment before placing his shot dead-centre between them.

He felt a little shaken: it wasn't the first man he had given a quick death to – the war saw to that – but it had never sat easy with him, coldly and deliberately ending a man's life. In the heat of battle or a gunfight, it was different, but just looking into a man's eyes, pain-filled or burning with hate like the breed's: it wasn't a good feeling. He murmured, 'Guess even a snake like you ought to be farewelled from this life, Cherokee.' He touched a finger to his hatbrim. '*Adios*, it's a long ride to hell.'

He covered the body with rocks, then rode fast out of the canyon. He had no idea where he was headed now.

CHAPTER 4

LAST MAN STANDING

Having nothing special to do while he waited for the local mayor to meet with him about the forthcoming town celebrations – it had been in existence for 50 years next month – Clinton Gage had a few drinks in the big saloon on Main. He had noticed a lot of folk at the far end of the street and could hear shouting, laughter and music from a small brass band. The *thumpthump thumpthump!* of a bass drum volleyed at infrequent intervals.

'Some kind of fair on down there?' Gage asked the man next to him. The man didn't answer, buried his nose in the glass of beer. Gage turned to a more friendly face on his other side and asked the same question.

'Carnival's in town for the celebrations,' the man answered amiably enough. 'Travellin' medicine show, you know, painted old hags tryin' to pass themselves off as "exotic" dancers escaped from some Ay-rab's harem, but for a coupla bucks you can get 'em round the back of the tent and find out they ain't no different to Big-Bellied Bertha from the local cathouse. They sell snake oil that'll cure anythin' too, an' there's a boxin' troupe an' jugglers an' so on. They'll cash in on our celebrations and make a few bucks.'

Gage thanked the man and bought him a beer before leaving. He wandered down to the carnival ground and jostled his way through the crowds, mostly drunk or well on the way to it but in a good mood, just out to enjoy themselves. He found himself standing in front of a large tent with a faded banner across the front proclaiming:

Carson's Champions
The West's Finest Boxing Troupe
We Take On All Comers
And PAY FIVE DOLLARS
To any man who can go a Three
Minute Round with our Champion
KID FARGO

'That's right, gents,' bawled a sweating man in worn waistcoat and collarless shirt suddenly appearing on a plank underneath the banner, a megaphone to his lips. 'Five loverly dollars in U-nited States crisp greenbacks. Just three minutes with our champeen and if you're still on your feet by then the money's yours . . . Hey, there, big fella, how about you? You look pretty tough to me and fast on your feet. Come on up here beside me and let the folks see you . . . Now ain't he a fine figure of a man, ladies and gents? What's that, sir? You accept the challenge! Good for you. A round of applause for our first challenger. Now, you, sir! Want an easy five dollars? Sure you do, well, c'mon up an' let folks see you. . . .'

Within minutes, the spruiker had three beer-smelling cowpokes jostling each other on the plank, willing to stand up against the troupe's champion. The mob began yelling to see the champion himself and the man with the megaphone grinned, bellowed, 'And here he is, folks! Light-heavyweight champeen of Chicago, Illinois, The Michigan Mauler, The Lightning Bolt from Laramie, Wyoming, best darn boxer this side of hell itself, Kiiiiiid FARGO!'

To Clinton Gage's surprise, the man who pranced out on the plank, poking holes in the air with flashing fists and wearing a light dust-coat over a pair of tight-legged ankle trousers, was none other than the same one who had left him to die in the wilderness. More than a year ago now. . . .

'Fargo Trent,' he murmured half aloud and felt his hands knot into fists down at his sides.

Before he realized what he was doing, he was up on the plank with the other three challengers. He was surprised at himself but this was over-ridden by his burning hostility for this man who had left him to die and so condemned him to the brutal treatment he had received at the hands of Sheriff Dub Bracemore and Griggs, the deputy who had lost a brother during the Cricket Creek bank hold up. His full beard was missing but there was enough stubble to tell Gage he was not mistaken: Kid Fargo was none other than the outlaw Fargo Trent.

Fargo was speaking into the megaphone now, obviously a prepared speech, probably repeated at every session. '. . . And I have to say, folks, my knees ain't a-shakin' nor is my belly doin' somersaults, not at the sight of challengers like *this*!' His words were obviously calculated to get the challengers' danders up and he poked a finger into the chest of the first man, a trail-driver just in to spend his pay.

'One minute, twenty seconds, *amigo*, and you'll be asleep on our canvas floor.'

Carson stood to one side, licked a stub of pencil and wrote something in a small notebook. The trail driver threw a punch that Fargo easily dodged, shaking a finger in the man's face.

'Now, now, don't be in such a hurry. And you, my friend,' he said to the second man, 'I'll give you one minute even . . . Hey, hey, hey! No fightin' outside the ring! Calm down now, save your energy. Number three, well, I might be just a leeetle tired by the time I get to you so I'll give you a minute-and-a-half. Thank you for not throwin' a punch *amigo*, I'll go easy on you.' Of course, nicely calculated, this *made* the man throw a punch which Fargo once again easily dodged and then he was face-to-face with Gage.

His expression froze, mouth half open, megaphone half raised. There was no doubt he recognized the man.

'You better save some energy for me, mister,' Gage said quietly. 'I intend to turn you into a prime imitation of mince meat! I might just need more then three minutes to do it. But I'll donate the five dollars towards your medical bills . . . Trent!'

Fargo's eyes held Gage's cold stare a moment, then he turned to Carson who came bustling along the plank, sensing trouble. 'The hell's goin' on here, Kid?'

'I know this man, boss. He's got some kinda grudge agin me, wants to beat the hell outta me. No punches pulled.'

Carson's thick eyebrows arched and then he grinned crookedly. 'Hey! Long time since we've had us a good grudge match! Always stirs the crowd.' He snatched the megaphone from Fargo and turned to the crowd, then swung back to Gage. 'What's your name, friend? Quickly!'

'Clinton Gage and I. . . .'

Carson swung away, bellowing into the megaphone. 'Folks, we have us a special attraction! A real, bone-bustin' grudge match! This here challenger, Killer Gage, has an old score to settle with my champeen, Kid Fargo. Now I'll tell you what I'm gonna do, these here three men have challenged in good faith so they will get their fights with The Kid. Win or lose, they'll get two dollars – yeah, I said *win or lose!* Then Fargo will have an hour's rest and . . .' He fumbled out a pocket watch and squinted at it, 'at precisely two o'clock this afternoon we will see the grudge match of the century! Kid Fargo versus Killer Gage! No limit! That's what I said folks, no limit. It finishes when only one man's left standin' and it'll be Winner Take All! I'll make the purse interestin' enough, say a fifty-dollar gold piece to the winner.' He lowered his voice a little. ' 'Course, there'll be side bets and I'll be on hand to take 'em and give good odds to those interested. . . .'

He stopped as Gage stepped forward and shook his

arm.' Listen, I'm not interested in making an exhibition of myself! I have something to settle with this man of yours and all I want is a chance to take a few swings at him and put him in hospital!'

Carson beamed. 'You hear that, folks? Now that's confidence for you! Misplaced, mind, but this man just wants a chance to put my champeen in *hospital*!' There was a burst of forced laughter through the talking cone. 'Oh, dear me! I can hardly talk for laughing! Friend, you'll get your chance. At two o'clock this afternoon. . . . That's the deal.' The voice lowered again and the beady eyes roved quickly to make sure no representative of the Law was within hearing. 'After you folks have a chance to get your bets set, eh? Why, we might all come out of this rich men! Except for the loser!'

And he aimed a confident, mocking grin at Gage. The crowd roared and clamoured for bets and Gage found himself pushed off the plank, the other three and Fargo hustled into the stuffy heat of the big tent for the first three matches.

Gage was angry but he wasn't going to pass up this chance just the same. If he had to make an exhibition of himself in order to take his revenge on Fargo Trent, then so be it.

He was ready!

It was a fight they still talk about in that town.

Fargo had underestimated Gage, too. He had never thought of him as being a tough guy, although he did have the recollection of the man seeming a lot fitter than his clothes and manner suggested.

Initially, he dodged most of Gage's blows but when

the first solid one landed, Fargo not only went down, he also skidded across the canvas square laid on the ground, bordered with loose ropes to form the 'ring'. His head was under one of these ropes and he looked up into the beet-red face of Carson.

'You got a bloody nose! Christ, man, that ain't good! The crowd want blood, but you make sure it's on the *other* feller!' A heavy boot cracked against Fargo's ribs and the impact thrust him back onto the canvas square. The crowd was yelling, screaming, a lot of men waving their betting slips. Fargo was abused and while Gage wasn't a local boy, he had the crowd's favour because Fargo had laid out all three local men earlier in the day. It was time for revenge and they wanted to see the colour of Fargo's blood, lots of it.

He clambered to his feet, Gage staying back. Carson grinned around his cigar as he tossed Fargo a damp cloth to mop his face. 'He's a walk-over! One of these idjuts who fights by *rules*, for Godsakes! Carry him a little, get the crowd excited and heated, then beat the crap outta him!' His voice hardened. 'You lose and you're through here!'

'Just knew you'd be backin' me up, boss!' Fargo panted. 'What lousy odds did you give me?'

'Get in there and wallop that dude!'

That was Fargo's intention, but it was easier said than done. Gage had obviously had lessons in proper boxing. He knew how to use the ring, not like these half-drunk challengers Fargo met wherever they travelled. He danced in and tapped and poked punches into Fargo's face and danced back again so that Fargo's retaliatory swings missed by a mile. Gage was the crowd's favourite and they roared encouragement.

Fargo's face was sore and swelling. He had been unconsciously holding back because it had troubled his conscience all this time about abandoning Gage in the badlands. Now he realized he was going to be beaten to a pulp unless he regarded this man as a true enemy and a thought came stampeding into his head that fixed Gage as not just hostile, but as a truly dangerous opponent. Because Gage knew his identity and that he was a wanted man. *Gage held his whole future in those big fists. . . .*

Fargo moved his head an inch to the left as a whistling right grazed his cheek and his hands came up, parried the follow-up straight left as he stepped in and drove a knotted fist into Gage's midriff. It was a well-fed midriff and softer than the rest of the big man. His breath *whooshed* and he grunted and sagged at the knees. The crowd yelled encouragement to Gage.

'Come back, Killer!'

'Hit him! Hit him, you damn fool!'

'Headbutt the sonuver!'

'Knee him in the balls!'

Carson shouted something about 'outside the rules' but got a lot of abuse in return. These men had seen one of their townsmen put in the local infirmary with a shattered jaw due to one of Carson's 'boxers' dropping on the man with a knee when he was sprawled on the blood-spattered canvas. So they weren't about to listen to anything said about 'rules' that might favour Fargo.

But the fighters themselves had been trading blows while the shouting was going on and, in the end, it was they who made the rules, which amounted to no rules at all.

47

While still doubled over, Gage rammed forward, driving his head into Fargo's belly. The outlaw grunted and lost some breath and his balance. Staggering back, doing a quick-step dance in an effort to keep his feet, he sprawled against the sagging rope and his upper body actually fell into the crowd. Rough hands clawed at him, landed a couple of punches, shoved him back like a catapult to meet a cracking roundhouse from Gage.

He went flying back, over the loose ropes, and landed in amongst the crowd again, only this time he was at their feet and dusty boots belonging to those who had bet against him – the majority – stomped at him and he covered himself desperately with arms and hands.

Carson lunged in with one of his bouncers and cleared the decks. They literally threw Fargo back into the ring, Carson growling, 'Finish the bastard, damn you!'

By then Fargo was ready to bust a few heads and he turned on Carson and the bouncer, smashed the latter across one cauliflower ear and sent the man yelling and swearing into the mob. Then he looked at Carson who started to back away hurriedly and Fargo stepped after him, reached across the ropes and dragged the promoter into the ring. Carson was flailing his not inconsiderable fists but Fargo dodged easily and gripped the grimy, greasy vest, hauled him close and head-butted him across the bridge of the fleshy nose. Carson dropped to his knees, wailing, blood squirting between his fingers. He floundered away on shaky knees, hands to face.

Gage stood watching, blinking in surprise, then Fargo bared his teeth at the man and ran across the ring, his body blurred he moved so fast.

'You son of a bitch! I *saved* your life by cauterizin' that wound!'

He punched Gage in the chest, followed with a cracking right to the jaw that sent the man spinning along the ropes, trying to keep his balance.

'And this is how you thank me, huh!' Fargo followed the words by grabbing Gage's shoulder, pulling him half-upright and driving a fist into his face. Gage's knees sagged and he dropped awkwardly, rolling away as Fargo kicked at him. Gage's face was dark with anger under the streaks of blood when he came lunging up.

'No rules now!' he gasped and Fargo had time to nod before the big body crashed into him and he stumbled backwards, arms raised to dodge the flurry of blows that flailed at his head and upper body.

Gage's weight carried him back into one of the ring posts and the wood splintered, leaning aside drunkenly as they hit. The post ground into Fargo's back and he gritted his teeth as breath gusted out of him. A blow took him on the side of the neck under his left ear and he spun away, once again fighting to keep his balance. Gage leapt in and a knee came up at his face. Fargo twisted aside and managed to take the blow, but from the man's thigh. It lifted him though didn't do any real damage and Fargo wrapped his arms about the leg, fumbled a grip and roared as he straightened abruptly, almost wrenching the leg out of its socket.

Gage somersaulted and landed face down against the rough, crumpled canvas sheet. Blood clogged his nostrils and there was a deep gash in his cheek, a flap of skin hanging. As Fargo closed, Gage's hands clawed at the creases in the canvas and he wrenched mightily. It was like pulling a rug out from under somebody's feet. Fargo crashed to the ground and in an instant Gage was on top of him, sledging blows down at his head and face. Fargo twisted and squirmed, using elbows and knees and bucking body movements to get out from under Gage and away from those heavy blows.

He tasted blood and felt his face slippery with it, wondered what shape his nose was in. It sure was damn hard to breathe through and most of his breathing now was through his parted, cut and swollen lips.

A forearm came down on his throat and he instantly slid back sufficiently to get Gage's weight across his upper chest bone rather than on his soft larynx. It caught Gage unawares and his arm slid away, his body following to one side. In an instant Fargo's fists smashed into the man's exposed armpit and he heard – and felt – the jarring impact followed by a heavy grunt of pain. Fargo lifted his knees, slammed Gage away. Both men rolled to their hands and knees and stood groggily, swaying, Gage's torn face dripping blood onto the ground from his bruised jaw.

The noise of the crowd was dim and distant by now, the fighters' heads roaring with thundering blood and pain.They saw the contorted faces and the working mouths, the shaking fists, the urging hands cupped around the mouths of those who had bet on one or the other. Carson wasn't in sight, nor was his bouncer.

Not that it mattered, the fighters had only eyes for

each other and their vision was not too good, either. Both had swelling, bruised eyes and they wiped the backs of sweaty hands across them in attempts to clear blurring vision. Fargo knew the secret of successful fighting was to keep moving, carry it to the opponent, give him no chance to recuperate or draw down a decent breath, for oxygen was all important at this stage.

So Kid Fargo lunged and hammered such a barrage into Gage that the man was carried back over the ropes, which now dragged on the ground and into the crowd. It became a mêlée but the fighters managed to stay in there slogging at each other, battering a path through the crush until they burst through the doorway of the tent, tearing the canvas, and spilled out into the carnival ground.

The crowd surged after them roaring, ripping the tent apart in their hurry to see the outcome. Tent poles were wrenched out of the ground and the canvas collapsed, trapping more than half the crowd. The din was worse than an Apache beer-bust on their deadly *tiswin*.

Fargo and Gage were rolling in the grass now, kicking away, staggering upright, trading punches that seemed as if they were holding a sack of wheat in each fist, the blows moved so ponderously. They circled with heavy hands dangling.

'Give . . . up!' Gage panted, landing one lucky blow that sent Fargo staggering drunkenly. He followed, making an obvious effort to lift aching arms, fists dripping blood.

'Like . . . hell!' Fargo gasped back, swung with all his

51

weight behind the blow, stumbling after the floundering Gage.

They grabbed at each other for support, sweating, bloody faces only inches apart. 'You left . . . me . . . to . . . *die*!' grated Gage but he had little breath to put much passion behind the words.

'Wish you . . . had . . . you . . . ungrateful . . . sonuver,' gasped Fargo in return.

They pushed away from each other, both swinging. Their arms tangled and they performed a crazy dance trying to unlock them, each pushing with his free hand against the other. It was more than they had strength for. Their knees gave way and they dropped, upper bodies falling against each other in mutual, if reluctant, support.

They continued to struggle ineffectually and then Fargo's eyes closed despite himself as fatigue overwhelmed him. He was carried to the ground by the dead weight of Gage who had already passed out, exhausted.

'Judas priest!' someone bawled. 'They's asleep on their feet!'

They awoke in separate cells, doused with cold water from a pail wielded by a stony-faced middle-aged man outside the bars. There was a lawman's star pinned to his old grey shirt. Spluttering, they sat up on the edges of their soaked bunks, holding their battered heads in their equally battered hands. Fargo could see out of one eye and then only if he squinted; Gage had a wide, white plaster and lint on one side of his face. He could see out of both eyes but had to hold the bruised, swollen lids up to do so.

'You don't look . . . too . . . good,' Fargo slurred, inside his mouth cut and swollen and tasting bloody. There was a loose tooth or two as well.

'Better 'n . . . you, I . . . bet!'

'Now, boys, fight's over. Shake hands and be friends!' The sheriff chuckled at his own joke. 'You are a mess!'

'Did I get the . . . fifty bucks. . . ?' slurred Fargo.

'Hell, why should . . . you?' Gage croaked. 'I . . . won!'

'The hell you . . . did. . . .'

'It was a draw,' growled the lawman, still amused by the state of the battered men. 'It was the last time Carson brings his so-called boxing troupe to this town, too.'

Fargo blinked. 'You kickin' him out?'

'He's long gone, him and all his hangers-on.' The man winked. 'He wants to run a bettin' book, he arranges my commission first.'

Fargo felt a chill in his belly. 'What do I have to do to catch up with him? I got a little money, but. . . .'

'I'll take your money, call it a fine,' the sheriff said happily. 'You ain't gonna need it, 'cause you ain't goin' nowhere, mister.'

'What the hell? I was just doin' my job!'

'Sure, but you were fightin' outside the confines of Carson's tent. Breach of the peace, friend. And. . . .' The sheriff gestured through the bars at Gage. 'Your good friend, Mr Gage, here, came round before you, or sort of part-way while the doc was stitchin' that gash in his face, had to give him a whiff of that there chlorry-form stuff. Man kept sayin' at last he'd caught up with the feller who left him for dead in the badlands somewheres, an outlaw named Fargo Trent!'

Trent went cold all over, his skin prickling. He turned his one good eye on Gage. 'You lousy son of a bitch!'

Gage shook his head quickly, then grabbed it firmly, regretting the movement, 'I, I don't recall that!'

'Likely not. You was under the chlorryform. Doc says you'd be surprised at what folk talk about while they're under, better'n a priest hearin' confessions, he reckons.'

'But a lot of that stuff is just part of crazy dreams under the anaesthetic,' Fargo said desperately.

The lawman allowed that was correct. 'But with you already callin' yourself "Kid" Fargo, I went to my bottom drawer which I hardly ever open and what you think I found?'

Fargo Trent sagged on the bunk. The lawman chuckled.

'Wanted dodger with a picture of you, Trent, with and without a beard: some artist feller doctored it. You mayn't resemble that picture too much right now, but there's enough for me to hold you while I look into your background some more. Carson don't know nothin', he says, and for once I believe him. So, you're gonna be my guest for a spell till I send a wire to Cricket Creek and get Sheriff Bracemore up here to positively identify you.' The lawman winked again. 'Cricket County's payin' a bounty on any member of that bank-robbin' gang.'

Fargo's battered face tightened and his eyes glinted as he looked through the bars at Gage. 'Thanks a lot!'

Gage spread his arms. 'I'm sorry, Trent, really. I

would've been content with beating you in a fight.'

'The hell you would've! You hate my guts!'

'I did, yes, I admit that, but twice you said that cauterizing my wound saved my life, well, I suppose it did. I'd never thought of it like that. Just remembered you'd abandoned me. I'm not sure I would have knowingly given you away.'

'We'll never know now, will we!' Trent said bitterly. 'You just better stay outta my reach!'

'Now, boys, you settle down. You, Mr Gage, can leave whenever you feel up to it. Trent, you behave or you'll have a few more wounds for the sawbones to tend to before Dub Bracemore gets here.'

'What happens then?' Fargo asked.

'Why, I collect my bounty, he takes you back to Cricket Creek and you hang.' The sheriff grinned. 'You won't be the last man standin'; you'll be the last man *swingin*!'

CHAPTER 5

THE FIREWORKS MAN

A week passed and Fargo Trent's injuries gradually healed, bruises faded, cuts scabbed over, aches and pains diminished as the days passed.

There was excitement in the town: fifty years old and celebrations were planned and performed each night. It was to culminate on the Saturday night, the actual anniversary of the proclamation of the first settlement in Drumhead Basin officially becoming a town. Drumhead lived up to its name with many drums beating at almost any hour of the day or night. There was singing in the streets too, mostly drunken.

People flocked in from all over for the fair and bunting and flags and big long tables of food were part of the enticements. There was to be free beer for two hours Saturday afternoon and Sheriff Andy Quinnell was not happy at the thought. He employed three extra temporary deputies in preparation for the expected influx of drunks.

'They'll mess up my cells, so bend your gun barrels over a few heads, drag 'em into an alley and let 'em sleep it off. Save us a lot of trouble. No real rough-stuff mind, or whoever gets carried away like that *will* be carried away after I've finished with him.'

'Still short-handed, Andy,' one man complained.

'There're three of you, my reg'lar deputy, Ray, an' me, we'll manage. Oh, and keep an eye out for that Dub Bracemore, the sheriff of Cricket Creek. He oughta be arrivin' any time.'

'Mebbe he could lend a hand?' the worried deputy suggested and Quinnell shrugged.

'Mebbe, I don't know the gennl'man so don't count on it. Now go catch some shut-eye and you be back at my office by sundown and we'll go through it one more time.'

Sometime during the afternoon, Quinnell remembered to bring some lunch for Trent who was lying on his bunk, belly growling. It was only cold beef sandwiches and tepid coffee, but better than nothing. The sheriff leaned on the cell door as Trent ate hungrily.

'When's Bracemore comin'?' the prisoner asked.

'Just had a wire. He won't be comin'. Sendin' someone named Griggs. Arrive mebbe today or tomorrer.'

'Listen, s'pose I tell you I had nothin' to do with that bank robbery?'

'S'pose you do. I won't believe you. Might if Griggs don't identify you, but till then you're the wanted man on that dodger. Now don't you gimme any trouble today or tonight, mister. Or you'll sleep through the fireworks with a knot on your head the size of a melon.'

'You're all heart, Quinnell.'

'I got worries.' The sheriff took the plate and cup and locked the door before moving away to his office.

Trent watched him go, then took out his dwindling supply of tobacco and papers and built a slim cigarette. He was all knotted up inside. There was nothing he could do. He had had only a few dollars to his name and they had gone to pay his 'fine'. Carson owed him close to a hundred but he knew he would never see that now. He suspected Quinnell might be open to negotiations, but he had nothing left to offer the man now. All he could do was sit in this damn cell and wait for Asa Griggs to arrive.

Ray Martell, Quinnell's permanent deputy, a man in his fifties with a game leg and one shoulder higher than the other, had told Trent when he asked that Clinton Gage was still in town.

'We sure's hell need him,' Martell said, old eyes lighting up. Trent suspected the man was a mite addled, not quite as mature mentally as he should be. 'He's the fireworks man! Gonna put on a show for us, light up the sky an' the prairie with whizz-bangs and pinwheels, rockets too! She's gonna be a good'n. Say, you'll have a pretty good view through the cell window. Stand on your bunk.'

It puzzled Fargo. 'The Fireworks Man? Clinton Gage?'

Then Gage appeared at the door of the cell just before sundown, bringing Trent a jug of frothing beer, getting it through the bars without spilling too much.

'The sheriff said you could have your share of the free beer. Don't cost him a thing.'

'Thanks.' Trent drank a great draught and smacked his still cut and swollen lips. 'What's this about you and the fireworks?'

Gage, still wearing a taped patch of lint over his stitched-up wound on his left cheek, smiled. 'That's my job.'

'Lightin' firecrackers?' Trent was sceptical.

'We-ell, Bracemore mistook me for you when he found me in the badlands, as you know. I told him I worked for Trans-Continent as a sort of searcher, scouting locations for their projects. I was working on that big Three Rivers holding-pen site for Silverton, in Missouri, when they nabbed me. Then I lost my job.' His face hardened. 'Thanks to you.'

'Me?'

'Yes. It took a damn long time for Bracemore to finally decide I was telling the truth, but T-C cancelled my contract. Said I'd given the company bad publicity.'

'Hell, not your fault!'

Gage shrugged. 'They saw it differently.'

'Not worth workin' for people like that.'

'I finally decided that, too. I was pretty much at a loss. I'd spent a couple of years out here in the west after throwing in my job as accountant for a fireworks company in Philadelphia. I sort of specialized. Wasn't qualified for much more than a glorified clerk, but I was good with figures and had a natural talent for finding locations that suited Trans-Continent's ideas. Not much brain-power involved but a lot of interesting travel.'

'Figured you for a greenhorn.'

Gage smiled crookedly. 'I had to struggle hard at

throwing off that tag! I happened to mention once I'd worked at a fireworks factory, studying the ingredients and formulae, so as to get a better idea of costing, I was applying for a shopkeeping job in Century Hill at the time and someone in authority thought it would be a good idea if they had a fireworks show to celebrate the opening of the railroad to the town. . . . Asked me if I could do it. Well, it was a big job but I had plenty of time and I knew what to do and what I needed, so I said OK.'

'And you been doin' it ever since?'

'Well, no, just now and again. I have quite a few contacts from when I worked for T-C and a connection with a man who had left the Philadelphia fireworks factory to start a small one of his own in St Louis. We did a deal. When I get the chance to put on a show, I contact him and we plan it out, and he ships me what I need and we share the profits. In between I've worked as tallyman at Abilene and Dodge cattle-yards, found a few odd accounting jobs, washed dishes but I like the outdoor life best.'

'Someone toughened you up since that night I found you,' observed Trent. He rubbed his jaw gingerly, smiling crookedly.

'Oh, that, my father taught me what he called the "manly art of fisticuffs" out of a book by some English Marquis. I did brush up on it a bit when I came West, but I don't like violence.' Gage seemed embarrassed, gestured to the cell window. 'You'll be able to see the fireworks in a couple of hours.'

Trent nodded. 'You're too kind, but I could do without watchin' it through a barred window.'

Gage was sober now. 'Look, Trent, I'm sorry about giving away your identity whilst under chloroform. I couldn't help it. I don't think I would've done it willingly.'

Fargo shrugged. 'Aah, I know it was just bad luck. *Mine!* Damnit! I just hope Griggs don't arrive yet a while.'

'Does he know you? I mean, he and Bracemore mistook me for you.'

'Well, that's easy enough to savvy: you had a wound, my jacket with mudstains, no horse or identification, a beard, and you were in the general area where they lost me. Griggs'll know me well enough. He won't've forgot his brother was killed in the hold up, either.'

'I see. Can't say I ever heard of any of the rest of your gang being captured. . . .'

Gage broke off as voices came down the passage and Trent looked up from his bunk as Sheriff Quinnell appeared with another man beside him, a solid-looking man with a drooping frontier moustache, hard-eyed and with a general bleakness about him. He looked only too familiar to Trent.

Gage turned as Quinnell said, 'Old friend of yours arrived in town just in time for the celebrations, Trent. You recall Sheriff Asa Griggs from Cricket Creek?'

Trent came up off the bunk now, absently grinding out his cigarette butt beneath a boot as he squinted closely at the man standing beside Quinnell, staring levelly at him through the bars. There was a tin star pinned to the man's worn leather vest and his right hand rested on his gun butt.

'Yeah, I recall him. Was only a deputy then.'

Gage's mouth was agape as he looked quickly at Trent who made a slight movement of his head side-to-side as the newcomer said, 'Well, the light in here ain't the best but it's good enough for me to recognize you, Trent, you murderin' scum! And I'll be happy to take you back to Cricket Creek and see you swing.'

Trent walked close to the bars and locked gazes with this man Asa Griggs. 'Guess I knew you'd catch up with me sooner or later, Griggs.'

The man grinned crookedly. 'Never doubted it for a minute, *amigo*.' He turned to Quinnell. 'Well, you got yourself the bounty, Quinnell. Ain't quite sure what it's gonna be. Think the biggest money'll be paid for Tag Benedict, but this sonuver's second on the list. I'd say you'll pick up the best part of a thousand.'

Quinnell straightened and whistled through his teeth, baring them in a wide grin. 'Well, I won't argue none about that! And call me "Andy", Asa. Now Trent's safe and sound here, how about I take you down to where they're passin' out free beer and we'll have our share?'

'Beer? Kinda weak for celebratin' such a windfall, ain't it, Andy?'

'OK! You're on! Let's go have us a few whiskies as chasers! You wanta join us, Gage?'

Griggs turned swiftly, looking closely at Clinton Gage for the first time in the deep shadows of the passage.

'Gage? Ain't you that feller was mistook for Trent?' The hand was on the butt of the sixgun now as Gage looked at him and nodded jerkily.

'You ought to know. You're the one took me in with Bracemore.'

Griggs nodded slowly, staring with cold eyes. 'So I was. Din' recognize you in this light. Yeah, why don't you join Andy and me for a little celebration? Hear this Trent gave you somethin' of a beatin'. You'll be glad to see the back of him.'

Gage grinned. 'You're right there. I'll come along, but I won't be able to do much drinking. I'm the fireworks man. One mistake and this town could go up in flames, or be blown off the map.'

'You never told me that!' Qunnell said, wide-eyed.

Gage shrugged. 'It can happen, but I take strict precautions, Sheriff. You go have your fun. I better go set up the show. It'll be dark soon and we don't want to keep the kids out of bed for too long.'

He glanced at Trent whose face was unreadable, and Griggs looked through the bars at the prisoner.

'Have to get back to Cricket Creek, Trent. I'll watch the show and then I think we'll hit the trail.'

'Tonight?' Quinnell frowned, startled.

'Long ride up here from Cricket Creek, Andy. Be a longer one goin' back with this bastard in tow.'

'You could get the noon stage south tomorrow.'

'Well, might consider that. Let's go see how much free booze we can put away. I can afford to risk a hangover if there's a stage available tomorrow.'

The man nodded to Trent and ushered Gage ahead of him, both men behind Andy Qunnell who was leading the way out eagerly.

Trent watched them go and walked slowly back to his bunk. *Wonder what happened to the real Griggs?* he murmured to himself. 'Tag wouldn't take a chance comin' in here, posin' as that lawman if he wasn't sure

63

Griggs wasn't gonna turn up and surprise him and a lot of other folk.'

And he wondered what plans Tag Benedict had for Gage. Right now, Clinton Gage was the only man in town, apart from Trent himself, who knew the man calling himself Asa Griggs was not who he claimed to be.

And knowing Tag Benedict, Gage would be lucky to live through the night.

It sounded like the battle for Little Big Top at Gettysburg to Trent when the first fireworks rattled their series of explosions through the town. The noise drowned the brass band that was playing rousing national songs in the Town Square and also the fiddlers at the dance down by the barbecue pits.

But the cheers and cries and whoops of the townsfolk and visitors drowned out everything else.

They had never seen the like of the display. A model of a golden waterfall, not unlike the one in Oxbow Canyon just southwest of town, spurted falling streaks of light that splashed realistically when they hit the flat stones packed beneath them. Down by the creek there were two fountains arcing, bright blue and red 'water' reflected in the still surface, illuminating the weeping willows and a couple of skiffs full of shouting drunks. It added to the entertainment when two men fell into the creek and had to be rescued, dragged ashore, retching, plastered with mud.

Fiery, spinning pinwheels and wagon wheels with spurting Roman candles lashed to their rims were set up on tree stumps and even living trees. Firecrackers racketed like volleys of gunfire. Some jumping-jacks and whizz-bangs whistled as they chased screaming, laughing kids all round the food tables. Sparklers had been handed out, dazzled all those who saw them. The children, and some adults, waving them in bright traceries of light. Rockets *whooshed*, high into the air and fanned wide patterns of coloured stars that drifted to earth, some exploding with ear-splitting cracks.

The town of Drumhead had never seen anything like it. Clinton Gage had planned well and enlisted the help of eager townsmen and youths, giving each a set piece as responsibility, emphasizing that the timing must be right so as to make the overall effect continuous, the best possible.

The show held the town entranced and the streets were thick with a swirling, drifting fog of impenetrable smoke. Some folks' eyes stung and throats were rasped raw, chests tightened, and coughing could be heard all over but no one complained. The experience was too wonderful for that.

And in the middle of it, after checking with his enlisted helpers that they understood exactly what was required of them, Clinton Gage backed into the shadows by the sprawling livery stables and in a few minutes was hurrying away through the thick fog of smoke.

Fargo Trent stood on the bunk as Deputy Ray had told him and he had a fine view through his cell window. For a little while there he actually forgot about his predicament and lost himself in the wonder of the fireworks painting the summer night sky.

He spun quickly as he heard a key scrape in the lock of the cell door, stumbled and stepped down from the bunk. The barred door swung open with a clang and a man stood there in the opening, one hand holding the ring of cell keys, the other a sixgun. Asa Griggs.

Even before the man spoke, Trent knew who it was as intermittent light flashed into the cell as rockets and fireworks exploded beyond the cellblock window illuminating his blocky form.

'Gettin' a good view, Fargo?'

'Wondered when you'd be back, Tag. How'd you fool Quinnell into thinkin' you were Asa Griggs?'

'Showed him Griggs' papers. Bracemore's gone and Griggs was proud as hell to have papers tellin' the world he's sheriff of Cricket Creek.'

'And how did you come by them?'

Tag Benedict tugged at his drooping frontier moustache. 'We-ell, I still have our old contacts in the telegraph offices here and there. Been tryin' to locate you, through 'em, matter of fact, for more'n a goddamn year! Tapper Rice told me about Quinnell sendin' for Bracemore, and another friend told me Griggs'd be comin' so I waited for him.'

'You bury him or leave him to rot?'

Tag Benedict looked bleak at first, then smiled crookedly. 'We-ell, let's say there was a little blood on the papers I showed Quinnell, but I told him I'd had a nosebleed. He swallowed it: all he's interested in is the so-called bounty he thinks he's gonna collect on you.'

Trent sat down on the edge of the bunk but he was tense, watching Benedict warily. 'What are you interested in, Tag?'

'Well, thought I'd take the opportunity while the whole blame town's watchin' Gage's fireworks to come and ask you somethin' I been dyin' to ask ever since we split up.'

'Well, if that's why you sent Cherokee to wait for me at the rendezvous, you made a mistake. He still held a grudge from the time he reckoned I stole his horse. He tried to bushwhack me.'

'Ah! Wondered what had happened to him. He's no loss. One less to divvy-up with.'

Trent went rigid. 'You haven't divvied-up with the boys yet? After a year?'

'Oh they each got a small share of the cash but there weren't much.'

'There was s'posed to be $35,000! It's why we took the chance of blowin' that damn huge safe!'

'Uh-huh, but only about ten thousand was cash.'

Trent stood slowly, eyes steady on the outlaw leader. 'We figured it was all cash! You told us it was!'

Benedict shrugged. 'You recall there was half-a-dozen bags and a small leather satchel?'

Trent said nothing but his blackened eyes narrowed and he nodded slightly.

'Twenty-five thousand was in diamonds,' Tag told him. 'Diamonds!'

'Uh-huh.' Tag watched Trent closely now. 'Chuck found out from Pete before he killed him we were s'posed to only take the cash. But I figured a leather satchel wouldn't be kept in a safe strong as that one if it only had a few papers in it. So I took it to make sure. And Pete was right.'

'But diamonds! How the hell. . . ?'

'You recollect who owned that mine at Cricket Creek?'

'Some company with a queer name, Vell or Felt or somethin' like that.'

'*Veldt*, South African Dutchies. They aimed to branch out into gold-minin', sent the diamonds to pay for a hammer mill and a separatin' plant, the way they do it in Africa, I guess. Cricket Creek bank is part of some international bankin' group and was gonna handle the deal and one of the Dutch engineers was comin' to set up the plant. But that part don't matter.' Tag paused here, walked slowly forward, gun steady in his hand now, cold gaze on Trent's battered face. '*You* picked up the damn satchel after we collided! Ran off with it! And I want it back!'

He lashed out with the gun unexpectedly and Trent felt the blow in his ribs like a wild horse had kicked him. He staggered, the edge of the bunk caught the back of his knees and he fell sprawling. Benedict stood over him, gun raised again, ready to club him.

'What'd you do with it, Fargo?'

'I lost it.' The gun raised threateningly over Trent but he didn't flinch. 'You think if I had diamonds, I'd be gettin' my head beat in every night for a few bucks?'

Tag frowned, then, without lowering the gun, nodded gently. 'I know how tough you can be, seen it time and time again in the war. You coulda hid it, in case there was a big hue 'n' cry. Takin'a miserable job as tent fighter'd be somethin' you'd do as cover. Go back later to collect the stones.'

Trent shook his head again. 'Hell, Tag. . . .'

That was as far as he got. He lunged forward, arms around Tag's hips, carrying him back against the bars. The breath gusted from the outlaw leader, but he was tough as an iron stove and even as Trent lowered his head to butt him in the midriff, Tag Benedict brought up a knee in a snapping motion.

It took Trent in the forehead and knocked him sprawling. He clawed at the bars to keep from going all the way down and then Tag was in front of him, gun cocked, the barrel pressing under Trent's right ear.

'We'll go someplace where we can talk in private! I'll shoot your knee caps off if you gimme trouble, Fargo. A gunshot ain't gonna be heard in this town tonight. You comin'?

Trent, groggy, ears singing, had no choice. Tag had horses waiting and he lashed Trent's wrists to the saddlehorn. Benedict mounted and motioned for Trent to move on ahead. He kicked his heels into the nervous mount's flanks and while the fireworks continued to bang and hiss and whoosh in explosive rainbows over Drumhead, the two men cleared town unseen.

Except by one man who stepped out of the shadows across the street.

Clinton Gage.

CHAPTER 6

LONG RIDE TO HELL

Tag Benedict must have had it all planned well ahead of time, likely spent a day or two scouting around Drumhead and the Basin, picking his trails and hide-aways should they be needed.

Both men's throats were thick with the aftertaste of powder smoke from the fireworks and Tag even remarked that it was just like a battlefield.

'That's what it is, ain't it? To you, Tag, it's always been a battlefield, you agin the world.'

Benedict laughed harshly, reached across and back-handed Trent, rocking him in the saddle. 'Mite philo-sophical for you, Fargo!'

'True, though.' Fargo Trent spat a little blood from a cut inside his cheek.

'And you? What kept you with the rest of us for so long?'

'Honestly don't know, Tag. Guess I liked the excitement after all those years in the war, livin' on our nerves and wits, mostly doin' whatever we liked. Civilian life looked mighty boring from where I stood.'

Benedict sounded wistful when he spoke. 'Ye-ah, dull as a wooden sword. Felt the same way, but figured I'd given all those years to the Confederacy and hadn't been paid one dollar for it. Had to be some sort of reckonin' and the Yankees seemed the best targets. Ripe for pickin'.'

'Till towards the end there: Cricket Creek ain't exactly in Yankee territory. Nor were two or three other places we hit. Or that train takin' repatriated Southerners back, for instance, carryin' a slew of money to set 'em up on land. Just Yankees tryin' to win co-operation durin' the Reconstruction after all the trouble they were havin', but the money was for helpin' Southerners.'

'An' it did; it helped us!' Tag looked bleakly at him though it was getting harder to distinguish features now they were riding into heavy timber in the hills above the Basin. 'It was Yankee money any way you look at it. 'Sides, you didn't have to come on the raid.'

Trent laughed briefly. 'No? I'd be a bag of bones under some cutbank long ago, if I hadn't.'

'True,' admitted Benedict. 'But you ran with us a long time, Fargo. You're damn handy with a gun, a mite slow to kill, but a damn good man to have around in a bind.'

Trent remained silent for a time, then said quietly, 'Well, I'm tired of bein' gallows bait, Tag.'

Benedict took his time replying. 'Does get mighty wearisome at times, I admit.' That surprised Trent but he remained silent. 'But what the hell has someone like me or Chuck or Sampson, hell, come to that, what've *you* got to look forward to even if you did manage to go straight?'

'Still workin' on it. It's damn hard. Not as much loose change to throw around. If it's a proper job, you got to watch the clock, someone tells you what to do.'

'Aaah, hell, yeah! That's why I ain't interested. So I'll run into lawman's lead some day. Or maybe I'll be back-shot by some sneaky bounty hunter. What the hell? While I'm alive, I'll enjoy myself.'

'Like I said, it's hard. I hunted buffalo after Cricket Creek for a spell, near Silverton, Missouri. That was OK, pretty good life, workin' with Injuns who did most of the skinnin' and fleshin', but it was a bloody job, Tag. Blood under your fingernails all the time, bits of rotten flesh, too, you stank of death. Kept remindin' me that buffalo weren't the only things that could die. Had a couple ranch jobs, not bad, but last man on is the first laid off come winter. Then I was broke, stood up to fight Carson's champion and broke his jaw with my second punch.'

'Yeah, you always did have hard knuckles.'

'He gave me a job, but it was too tough, gettin' your head hit every night. I'd've been punch-drunk in another month or so. Carson owes me near a hundred bucks, but I guess I'd have to fight *him* to get it. . .' He paused briefly.

'Hundred bucks? Hell, you'd've spent that in an hour after some of our jobs!'

'Well, I tried to get used to the idea of havin' mostly empty pockets but now I'm back where I started.'

Benedict's head swung towards him fast. 'Oh, no you ain't, Fargo. You're a long way from there. You ran out on the rest of us and you stole them diamonds. Mebbe after you tell me where you've got 'em stashed you'll be back with us. Mebbe not.'

'That's more likely.' Trent sounded bitter. 'Specially as I don't have any diamonds hid away and you're too damn cold-blooded, Tag, think about yourself too much and the hell with anyone else.'

'Only way to be, now shut up. I got some figurin' to do. Gotta find my way through these hills to where the rest of the boys are waitin'.'

Trent felt his heart lurch. It seemed to drop down into his stomach. That was just the kind of news he didn't need to hear!

They were all there, Chuck Keel, Old Sampson, Big Tom Santos.

They were gathered around a small fire in a hidden canyon not much bigger than a couple of livery stables pushed together. The entrance was good, narrow and brush-choked, then it opened out into flat ground with a few minor dips and cutaways. It rose slightly towards the back of the canyon and the outlaws had built their fire under the overhanging sandstone wall that was dotted with clumps of bush. There was brush curving around in front of the overhang, too, so it gave the camp a good deal of cover

Keel was the first one on his feet, walking across chewing on flame-seared rabbit he had just gnawed off a legbone. He tossed the bone away and wiped his greasy hands down his loose, grubby shirt-front. He looked meaner than ever, hard little eyes boring into Trent as the man sat there, hands numb and cut from being tied to the saddlehorn for so long on the rough trip up here.

Trent stiffened as Keel pulled his knife but the man merely sawed through the ropes. As Trent winced a little when the blood flowed painfully back into his hands and wrists, Keel grabbed his leg and heaved, tipping him violently off the horse, which pranced away with a whinny.

Keel moved in and drove a kick at the rolling Trent. It took him on the back of a shoulder and hurt, forcing a grunt of pain from the prisoner. Trent rolled onto his back and swung up his legs as Keel stepped in for another kick. Keel ran onto the riding boots and Trent kicked hard, rolling to one side so the worn and ragged high heels tore Keel's shirt – and his flesh underneath.

It took the man by surprise and he fell to one knee, putting down a hand swiftly to keep from falling all the way. It was his gun hand and Trent saw this, immediately lunged up and kicked Keel in the chest, his hands still leaden and more or less useless down at his sides. But as Keel rolled on the ground, winded, face congested, Trent knelt trying to grab Keel's sixgun.

He fumbled too much and Big Tom grabbed his shirt collar and effortlessly threw him into the brush. Keel staggered up, grabbing for his gun now, but Tag Benedict's voice lashed like a whip.

'Leave it! Save it for later. We need him right now.'

'Who needs him?' grated Keel but he relaxed some, rubbing his chest and his belly. His eyes were murderous. 'I'll be here, Trent! Here an' waitin'!'

'All right, settle down,' growled Benedict, tired and dirty, reeking of fireworks' smoke, and hungry.

He stepped to the fire where they had rigged a small spit made out of yew sticks, two forked, one laid across with the rabbit skewered on it. Benedict took up the whole stick and began to gnaw at what was left of the carcass.

'Hey, that's our supper!' complained Sampson. 'Judas, I ain't had hardly any. . . .'

'Then go out and shoot another one,' Tag said, continuing to eat, mouth full, bits of partly chewed meat spilling from his lips. He glanced at Trent. 'Hungry?'

'Not after seein' you eat. I'd almost forgot how it's turned my stomach all these years.'

Tag snorted and tore off another lump, crunching bones. The other outlaws looked miffed but no one tried to take the rabbit off Benedict. When he had finished with it, he tossed it carelessly away. There was still a little meat left on the bones, but it landed on the dirt near the fire and no one wanted it now.

Trent wouldn't have minded it, grit and all, he was that hungry, but he looked away from it, preparing himself mentally for what he knew must surely be coming his way from these men.

'Guess he didn't tell you nothin', or you wouldn't've brought him here,' Chuck Keel said, still glowering at Trent.

'Says he don't have the satchel – which, I might add, I believe. But he ain't yet said where it *is*!' Benedict smiled crookedly.

Keel asked irritably, 'Well, what the hell you been

doin' all this time while we been sweatin' it out up here?'

'Aw, Fargo an' me've had a philsophical discussion, sort of put things right with the Reconstruction an' the world in general.'

Keel, Big Tom and Sampson exchanged looks.

'Anyone know what the hell he's talkin' about?' Keel snapped.

Big Tom drawled in his Kentucky way, 'I think Tag's tellin' us Trent din' tell him nothin'.'

'Nothin' I believed, leastways,' Benedict said, face straight and hard now. 'But he will, won't you, Fargo? You'll tell us what we want to know and be glad to do it. You recollect what Cap'n Easy used to say to us before we went up agin big Yankee odds?'

'I do,' spoke up Sampson. 'He used to say, "C'mon, boys, cheer up. It's a long ride to hell!" ' He shook his head wonderingly. 'An' damn me, if we didn't just laugh and then cheer, cut loose with our rebel yells and go chop them Yankees to pieces!'

'We was hard bastards, wasn't we?' Big Tom opined.

'Tough as they come,' allowed Benedict, still watching Trent. 'That includes you, Fargo. Which means we got us some work to do on you, so we best get started.'

'Hold up!' Trent said quickly, massaging his hands and wrists, which were no longer numb, but he kept up the pretence. It never hurt to let your enemies think you were more incapacitated than you were. 'Look, I can tell you what happened but that's all I can do, because I dunno where the satchel is now.'

'You could make a guess, save yourself a heap of pain. A *heap* of pain,' Tag said quietly.

Trent was hunkered down by the bushes now, arms across his knees, absently rubbing his wrists and hands. There was nothing but hostility on the faces of the four men facing him.

'Tag, after we blew the safe, I grabbed a couple of canvas bags; you took bags and the satchel.'

'I knew what was in it, or guessed it was *somethin'* mighty valuable or it wouldn't've been in that vault.'

Trent nodded impatiently. 'Outside after that fellar at the buckboard was killed all hell was breakin' loose. It was raining, if you recall, I slipped in the mud, cannoned into you. . . .'

'You cannoned into me, then slipped in the mud,' Tag said coldly.

'If that's the way you recall it. . . .'

'Damn right it is! And I've played it over in my mind a hundred times since.' Benedict leaned slightly forward. 'Know what I decided, Fargo? That you *meant* to collide with me, grab the satchel and make a run for it. Or, if that didn't work and I dropped the satchel, which I did, you'd snatch it up with a couple of bags of money to make it look good, like you took it accidentally. . . .'

Tag let his voice trail off, face like an executioner.

'And you jumped aboard that grey of yours and got outta there like the devil himself was after you, *and* you made sure you separated from the rest of us, never showed at the rendezvous. . . .'

'I showed,' Trent said quietly. 'At all three and you had Cherokee waitin' at the third.'

'My mistake,' admitted the outlaw leader. 'Should've known he'd try to kill you. Never did forgive an' forget, ol' Cherokee.'

'I thought it was long past, that deal where we nearly got ambushed by a posse and I jumped on the first mount I could grab, happened to be his. Got it shot out from under me and he reckoned I owed him fifty bucks for it. Two years he kept hasslin' me about it.'

'Like I said, Cherokee never forgot a hurt. Anyway, my guess is by the time you showed at the rendezvous you didn't have the satchel with you any longer.'

Trent was slow to answer, knowing how it was going to sound. 'No, no satchel, no bags of coins.' They stirred angrily and he went on quickly. 'I was wounded, the grey was hit. It was just past the north end of Horsehead Pass and Bracemore's posse was comin' in the south end. There was a herd of buffalo near me. I was hurtin', the hoss was dyin', I rammed a handful of burrs under his tail, sent him into the herd with my blanket flappin' from the stirrups. The buffalo took off like they were tryin' to fly, must've scared hell outta the posse. The stampede wiped out my tracks, too.'

There was silence as his voice drifted off. Then Benedict said, 'And?'

'I was able to get away on foot and later found Gage lyin' wounded and took his mount. . . .'

'*Fargo!*' roared Benedict, making Sampson jump in fright. 'Goddamn you! We ain't interested in how you claim you got away. *What about the coin sacks and the satchel?*'

Fargo Trent sighed heavily, running his gaze around the grimfaced outlaws. 'Like I said, I was wounded, bleedin' plenty, afoot with hardly any water, no grub, light-headed. I guess I was in somethin' of a panic, Tag.'

There was another silence broken only by the small

snapping of burning twigs in the fire. Big Tom pushed some more wood into the flames.

'*You* panicked?' asked Tag Bendict softly. Trent nodded knowing how dangerous this moment was. Tag suddenly spat on the ground. 'So Fargo Trent panicked, the same Fargo who tackled four Yankees armed to the teeth while all he had was two shots left in his pistol and a bayonet. *That* Trent never panicked. He shot two Yankees dead, ran a third through with the bayonet, fought hand-to-hand with the other and broke his neck *then* blew up their cannon with an overcharge of powder and made his way back to our lines through a hundred Yankees scattered all over the hillside. And you're askin' us to believe this same man *panicked*, miles ahead of a posse, in a hassle, sure, but nothin' like some he had durin' the war and got outta them without missin' a draw on his cigarette.'

'It wasn't like that, Tag!' Trent cut in. 'For a start, I wasn't the same man as at that Hilltop battle. I'm ten years older now and I was wounded and had few chances of gettin' away.'

'But you thought things out coolly enough, tyin' a blanket to your stirrups, gettin' the burrs to start your hoss so a shot didn't give away your position.' This was Chuck Keel speaking, quietly, almost reasonably, but his eyes were burning with an urge to kill he was barely holding in check.

Trent nodded slowly. 'Yeah, but time was runnin' out. The posse was already in the pass by then, comin' fast. If the buffalo stampede didn't work, I was done for. I had hardly any ammo left.'

The others started all speaking at once but Benedict

brought them to order with a roaring curse. Looking as bleak as a blizzard, one hand on his sixgun butt, he spoke quietly to Trent.

'So the pressure was on and you panicked!'

Trent ran a tongue across his lips. 'I was just so damn anxious to get that grey runnin' in amongst the buffalo, Tag, that I forgot my saddlebags were still on its back. I'd thrown off my warbag and rifle and canteen, ripped up the blanket. . . .'

'We know all that. So you set your hoss in among the bison and he took your saddlebags with him. And I s'pose you're gonna tell us the coin bags and satchel were in those bags.'

'I know how it sounds, Tag, but that's gospel.'

The canyon was quiet again, only the fire crackling, the hostile stares raking Trent like Mexican gut-ripper spur rowels. Tag started tapping his fingers against the butt of his Colt, not taking his eyes off Trent. Keel was stirring restlessly, waiting for the word to start work on Trent, give him some encouragement to change his story, which as he had known and feared they disbelieved without hesitation.

'The grey, he ran right into the herd? Got trampled? Or did he get out to the fringe and just give out from his wound?' asked Benedict grimly, impatiently.

'He was trampled to mush in the stampede, Tag,' Trent told him quietly. 'A few buff went down too and they were no more than piles of chopped up meat. The grey wasn't even visible.'

'So you went back and looked, you son of a bitch!' snapped Keel starting forward.

'Wait, Chuck!' Tag stepped towards Trent as Keel

80

reluctantly stopped. 'Did you go back and look?'

'Like hell I did! I got outta there as fast as I could and that wasn't fast enough far as I was concerned. I was losin' blood, my boots were run-over, I had to pack my warbag and rifle. No, I rested on some high boulders on the slope above the plains leadin' into the pass. It was jammed with dead buffalo and there was no sign of the posse. They'd have to go clear round the range to get onto the plains then, but I saw how the ground was all churned up. Crows and buzzards were already at work on the dead buffalo. The grey was somewhere in amongst those carcasses, buried underneath. And that meant the cash bags and the satchel were trampled into all that bloody ground. And far as I know they're still there.'

'The pass would've been cleared out long ago,' Benedict said gruffly. 'Someone might've gotten lucky and found 'em.'

'What the hell you sayin'?' demanded Keel, narrow-eyed as he glared at his boss. 'You *believe* this crap he was talkin'?'

Tag shook his head, still looking at Trent. 'No, just pointin' out why his story does us no goddamned good, even if it is true.'

'Of course it don't!' Trent agreed belligerently. 'It does no one any good but that's what happened. And I told you on the way here, Tag, that I decided I didn't want to be gallows bait any longer. So I never gave any thought to goin' back to that pass. Hell, I didn't even know about the diamonds till you told me down in Drumhead! You played that one mighty close to your chest!'

'By Godfrey, but he makes it sound good, don't he?' opined Big Tom Santos, his Kentucky drawl more noticeable than ever like it always was when he was on edge, about to go into action or some kind of fight.

'He always did have the gift of the gab,' growled Sampson. 'Look how he could talk you into believin' he had a good poker hand! Many's a dollar I've lost to him through lettin' him bluff me!'

'I'll make him tell the truth,' Keel gritted.

Tag smiled thinly at Trent. 'You're between that rock and a hard place, Fargo, but your long ride to hell ain't started yet. Now's when we begin askin' you all over again and this time if you don't come up with the right answers. . . .' He shrugged, spread his hands. 'That trip to hell's gonna seem like it's never gonna end.'

CHAPTER 7

HELL

They beat him around a little but not too much. It wasn't that there was any lack of interest in what they hoped Trent would have to say but the outlaws all seemed tired and edgy.

It was Trent's guess as he lay there hog-tied hand and feet on stones under the overhang, that they were jumpy over the fact that Benedict had killed Griggs, a sworn deputy of the Law. And Tag himself wondered how Andy Quinnell was going to react when he realized he had lost his prisoner who was worth a thousand dollars to him. Or so he believed.

'Get some shut-eye,' Benedict said, panting some after having beat Trent for several minutes. He casually kicked the bleeding, semi-conscious man at his feet and looked at the others. Chuck Keel was especially eager to continue. 'Griggs don't bother me none: it'll be some time before anyone expects to hear from him but Quinnell's hungry for dollars and he might think I'm tryin' to pull somethin' by breakin' out Fargo.'

'You are,' Keel said bluntly and Benedict nodded.

'Yeah well, I figure we'll be better off if we up-stakes before daylight and get deeper into these hills. You know 'em pretty good, don't you, Sam?'

Old Sampson looked a bit dubious. 'Used to, long before the war I was up this way scoutin' for the wagon trains, but I ain't been here for years.'

'You find us a safe way through,' Tag Benedict said and it was an order.

Sampson looked worried but nodded. 'I'll do my best, Tag.'

'Better than your best, you'll *do* it!'

That didn't make Sampson happy and he took out his frustration by planting a kick against Trent's back before turning in.

Trent lay there, sore, throbbing from head to foot, realizing quickly that it was useless to struggle against his bonds. At least he would get a little break while they were travelling away from this place, for whatever good it might do. However small, the chance of some sort of recuperation would be welcome. For he knew he was going to suffer plenty and futilely, because he had no idea where the satchel of diamonds was. It must have been trampled underfoot by the buffalo stampede and the best he could hope for was that Benedict would go back there and look for himself.

It would only be a two or three-day ride, less for one man riding hard. If he saw Tag was wavering over the question of should he or should he not go back and look in Horsehead Pass, Trent decided to urge Benedict to send one man to do the job. That would be one less for him to worry about. Not that he had any kind of an escape plan yet, but it wouldn't hurt to cut down the odds if he could.

But, as he might have known, Tag Benedict wasn't about to trust *anyone* going to search for the diamonds unless he was along to supervise.

They broke camp early, the outlaws getting in a few good licks at him when they set him on his mount, hands still tied but legs left free to straddle the horse.

'Leave him be,' growled Tag as they rode away from the small canyon and Keel backhanded Trent in the narrow entrance. 'We'll find a place where we can really work on him.'

'Better not be too damn long!' Keel growled, glaring at Sampson. 'You hear, Sam?'

Sampson heard all right, heard the unspoken threat too, and his belly churned. 'I'll find a way through the hills, don't worry.'

He spurred on ahead, just to get away from the scowling looks thrown his way by Keel and Tag Benedict. The country looked vaguely familiar in parts, but he didn't recognize much. Hell, it was before the war when he had been pathfinder for the immigrant wagon trains through these hills. Timber had grown and changed the skyline, rains had eroded the slopes, silt had built up in draws he had once known, cutbanks had collapsed, creeks had overflowed and made new courses. *There had been too many changes!*

His mouth was dry. His heart hammered hard in his scrawny chest. He wished he had kept his mouth shut about once having known this area.

But Sampson had a lucky break: he recognized a swift-flowing stream and while it now lay further west than he recalled, he saw that it would still lead to a watering and camping place the old wagon trains had used.

'We follow this stream and we'll come to a place that oughta suit us just fine, Tag,' he told the outlaw leader happily. 'There's water, brush and rocks to give us cover and game in the woods. Easy for guardin', too.'

'Let's go then,' growled Keel and was about to spur away when Big Tom Santos drawled in his casual way, 'Reminds me of a crick back home. My pappy drug a couple revenue men up an' down it at the end of a rope, till they spilled their guts, told him where the rest of the agents were settin' up ambush, how many, every-thin'. 'Course they were almost drownded by then so after they talked, pappy finished the job an' we got our moonshine out safely, then went and jumped them revenue men. I was just a shaver.'

Keel wheeled his mount and his broken, stained teeth bared in a grin as he rammed his mount into Trent's sorrel. The horses both whickered and thrashed but didn't go all the way down. Not like Trent. His hands weren't tied to the saddlehorn so he sailed out of leather and hit the slope. He was still rolling when Tag looked hard at the grinning Keel who was unshipping his lariat.

'Why waste the time?' Keel said. 'There's the stream, there's Trent and here's my rope! We gotta follow the water anyway, accordin' to Sam, so let's work a little on Trent!'

He walked his horse into Fargo as the man staggered to his feet. Trent sprawled and Keel was out of the saddle swiftly, taking a couple of turns of rope around his ankles. Then he mounted, dallied rope around his saddlehorn and rode his horse into the shallows.

Trent bounced and spilled over the ground and splashed into the muddy water. Keel turned towards midstream and soon his horse was swimming. Trent's body followed and water foamed and surged over him, roared in his ears as his head went under, filling his nose and mouth.

He spluttered and coughed, trying desperately to grab a good lungful of fresh air. He got only a little and then the stream water flooded his throat again and he choked. At the end of the rope, his body twisted with the motion of the stream and the swimming horse. His head went under again. He kicked and bucked in an attempt to roll onto his back, to get his face above the surface.

He could hear nothing but the thunder in his head as Keel urged his mount on, turned it to where it could get footing in belly-deep water and raked with the spurs. Blood ran down the wet flanks and legs and the horse protested, but Keel kept raking and cursing, slapping its head with the sodden rawhide of the rein ends.

Trent's speed increased and he knew then he was going to drown if someone didn't kill this son of a bitch who was dragging him through the water. But the surge of hot anger was gone in a second as self-preservation took over, the adrenalin pumping as involuntary fear saturated his body.

The more he struggled, the more water he swallowed or choked on as it spurted up his nostrils. With a force of will he didn't know he had, or how long he could call upon it, he made himself relax on his back. It was a long way from being perfect, but it gave him some relief. He was actually planing, skimming along like this, plenty of water still washing around his head, covering his face frequently but there was respite as his body made its own passage and a sort of cavitation formed around his head, enabling him to breathe erratically. *Just breathing at all was some kind of victory.*

He hoped they wouldn't notice. Keel was being cheered on now as Trent concentrated on staying on his back, deliberately dunking his head under occasionally, coughing and spluttering to make it look worse than it was.

'Don't kill him!' called Tag Bendict as Trent began to sink when Keel's panting mount slowed down. 'You drown him, Keel, he's gonna have company!'

Chuck Keel scowled but he hauled in on the rope, pulling Trent into the shallows where the man rolled onto his side, vomiting muddy water, body shaken by racking coughs. Very little of it was an act but he did work at making it sound and look as bad as possible.

His exhaustion when he had finished coughing and vomiting was no act, though: he really was more than half-drowned.

'Give him some more?' Keel asked eagerly.

Tag didn't answer, squatted beside the sodden Trent, watching his chest heave as he still fought for air. 'You happen to recollect where that satchel might be, Fargo?'

It was some time before Trent could even speak a coherent word but he choked out a sentence or two they could savvy.

'Has to . . . be . . . where . . . buff . . . stamp . . . stampeded through . . . H . . . Horsehead . . . Pass. . . .'

Tag slapped his cold, wet face, more water spraying from Trent's gravel-clogged hair. 'We been through this before, damn you!'

Trent shook his head, gasping, trying to find enough breath to repeat what he had just said. It earned him another slap and, shortly after, another near-drowning in the river.

It took a long time for him to come round and Benedict was threatening to kill Keel if he had drowned Trent. But Fargo came to eventually, in a welter of gushing water and sand and choking words.

They came out just the same: Horsehead Pass. It was the only answer he could give. Keel was all for continuing the water torture but Benedict refused. 'Gainin' nothin'. I dunno how he could know anythin' about the diamonds, anyway, so he'd want to grab the satchel. Might've just figured somethin' valuable had to be in there, but . . . I'm beginnin' to come round to his way of thinkin'. If the satchel was in his saddlebags and the hoss was trampled in the stampede, there's only one place it could be.'

Keel didn't like it, though Big Tom seemed convinced and Sampson went along, anything to take the pressure of himself.

'Well, what's that mean?' growled Keel. 'One of us has gotta ride all the way back to Horsehead Pass for a looksee?'

'No damn way!' snapped Benedict. 'We all go look.'

'Hell, Tag! Someone could've found it by now, if it ever was there layin' on the ground!'

'Wouldn't be layin' out where it could be seen,' Big

Tom said reasonably. 'It'd be trampled underneath by all them buffalo.'

Keel spat. 'That pass has been in use the last year or so, *anyone* coulda come across it. Dust blowin' away so it showed a corner or somethin'. That's if it was ever there!'

'Possible,' conceded Tag. 'So we go and check.'

Keel's face was tight, his cheekbones showing, sunken and hollow, giving him a death's-head look. 'What about Trent?'

'Aw, he comes along, 'cause if we don't find that satchel, he's gonna find out what real hell is!' Tag laughed as he nudged Trent with a boot toe. 'OK by you, Fargo?'

Trent didn't even have enough strength left to reply so he merely nodded his head.

As if he had a choice!

It was a gruelling ride, Sampson getting lost twice when the stream took an unexpected bend and time was wasted back-tracking. The old man looked worried and Chuck Keel kept needling him, dropping a threatening hand to his knife hilt: they all knew Sampson's fear and abhorrence of cold steel. Ever since a Yankee bayonet had taken him in the chest at The Wilderness and the steel had missed his heart by an inch, he had nurtured a blood-chilling dread of blade weapons.

Keel grinned crookedly, knowing full well how his unspoken, though amply demonstrated, threats would upset Old Sampson.

'Gettin' senile, ain't you?' he threw back in passing one time. 'Forget your own name soon, you old coot.'

'I, I'll remember yours!' Sampsom croaked and Keel laughed again.

'Damn right you will!'

'Leave him, Chuck,' Benedict said with a hard edge to his words. Trent noticed how Keel stiffened, his face straightening, and the mocking grin disappeared pronto. 'He's doin' his best.'

'Ain't good enough,' Keel murmured, maybe not loud enough for Benedict to hear.

But the outlaw leader set his bleak gaze on Sampson. 'No more mistakes, Sam.'

'No, Tag, hell no! It's OK now – I know where we are.'

'Sure,' piped up Keel, unable to resist. 'But where are we goin'?'

Sampson led them to the place he had been seeking, where the old wagon trains used to bed down for a few days to repair their Studebakers and Conestogas, the women taking the opportunity to bake bread and cook joints of meat for the long trail that still lay ahead.

It was a pleasant place, the stream broadening, a curving beach of gravel, some deadwood in mid-water, weed strung out in languid tresses by the small current, like a maiden's hair. There were tall trees, short trees and brush as well as some boulders dotted around on the northern side. As Sampson had said earlier, it would be an easy place to guard.

One man in the boulders could see clearly on both sides for a long way. Blue-hazed hills rose steeply beyond in the south, a dark slash of a pass just showing.

Trent noted all this as he sagged in the saddle, held in place by his bonds. It was Keel of course who shoved him roughly so that he fell hard but the gravel was fine enough to cushion the fall a little. Sun rays slanted down through timber on the high ridge and a cool dark shadow crept over the campsite. Keel looked disappointed when Benedict told him to leave Trent be.

'We'll have supper, turn in early and start before sun-up again.'

'He needs a beatin' just to make sure he ain't joshin' us, Tag!'

Tag laughed. 'Look at him! Would you feel like joshin' someone who did that to you and was ready to start all over again if the joke backfired? He'll keep. We'll check out Horsehead Pass and if that satchel ain't there, could well be the end of the trail for Mr Fargo Trent.'

He looked at Trent who stared back with empty eyes. But he knew Tag was just talking: be no sense in killing him as long as they figured he knew about the satchel. But that likely wouldn't stop Tag, or Keel, if the notion took them and things got out of hand.

So the future didn't look so bright.

They gave him a drink of water but no food, and turned in soon after dark. There was a new moon, spilling little light from its thin crescent. The campfire died down and after Big Tom came back from the boulders, he was a cautious man was Tom Santos, and announced the all clear, snores soon drifted across the expanse of gravel, drowning the trickling of the stream.

Trent was aching, his mouth thick despite the water they had given him. There were cuts inside his cheeks and lips. One eye was swollen half-shut and the other was bloodshot and bruised. His hands were numb again but Tag had finally acceded to his request to have the bonds loosened slightly. There was nowhere near enough slack for him to work free. His ankles were still bound too, but his riding boots protected his flesh and so they were not numbed. But they ached like blazes.

He knew he had a lot more hell to face before they were finished with him. He knew deep down that they wouldn't find any trace of the satchel after all this time and that only meant more suffering for him.

But he near exhausted himself over the next two hours trying to get free. Finally, he just had to give up and let his battered body rest. . . .

He awoke to gunfire.

A raking, hammering volley, interspersed with a couple of whistling ricochets. The shooting was coming from the brush and also some more from across the stream amongst the boulders.

They were surrounded and whoever it was had no intention of playing by the rules. No one called a warning, or an order to throw down their arms. The shooting just began and turned the camp into chaos. Men were swearing as they rolled out of their blankets, groping for their weapons, blinking away the sleep as they rose to knees or crouched low, seeing the gun flashes in the brush and boulders.

'Goddamn posse's split up!' Tag yelled seeing the flashes on both sides of the stream. 'Git down behind that hump! Quick, if you want to stay alive!'

Keel hurled himself bodily over the hump in the gravel stretch, scrabbled round and began shooting back. Thick powder-smoke rolled in as the others dived for cover, three shooting into the brush, but Big Tom cutting loose at the boulders where there seemed to be less gun flashes. Then the ground-hitched horses started whinnying and prancing and moments later charged across the stream, down from the camp.

'Judas! There goes the broncs!' yelled Old Sampson.

He started to crab away from the rise, wanting only to get onto a horse and ride away from what he saw as a place that would be full of dead men in a few more minutes.

They had left Trent lying in the hollow near the line of brush where he had been dumped before they had turned in. Fargo was hunched down, but looking wildly from one side of the stream to the other. He saw the horses run off. The shooting was dying down a little now but still no one called out. Looked to him like this posse was only here to collect scalps and that would include his own, because he was still an outlaw in the eyes of Quinnell and his deputies.

His heart almost stopped as something darted out of the brush behind him and went for his legs. *Snake*, he thought and started to pull his legs up. But some weight held them and he felt movement between his ankles, waiting for the hot needle sensation of fangs penetrating his leather boots or teeth from some bigger animal ready to crunch bone.

It was neither. It was a knife blade and the steel severed the bonds, freed his ankles. In seconds his hands were free too, and the painful return of blood made him bite his lips and moan involuntarily.

His silent rescuer dragged him half erect by his shirt-front, ducked and put him over his beefy shoulder, backing off into the brush. Trent croaked a question that wasn't answered and then they entered the pall of smoke, which hid them both from the outlaws. Even as they disappeared into the smoke, the 'shooting' died away desultorily and Sampson jumped up again in what he figured was a lull and began to run after the horses, shouting.

'Get down, you idiot!' bawled Benedict but Sampson kept running.

Keel started up, snarling loudly, 'Christ! We been flim-flammed! That was goddamn fireworks, not guns! Smell the smoke! It's different!'

The outlaws froze, except Sampson. Then from the brush there was a rushing sound and several trails of fire streaked across the sand. There were two explosions against the boulders, briefly lighting up the camp. Then Sampson screamed as the third rocket found him and burst against his thin chest. The sounds he made chilled the blood of the others and they froze, watching Old Sampson turn into a human torch, running wild, hands beating at his blazing clothes and hair, until he finally fell into the stream. There were hissings and feeble thrashings, then silence as his body bobbed up and down and a sickening stench in the smoke-laden night.

The last firework made a fizzling sound and several small fires started in the line of brush, quickly taking hold and rearing into a blazing wall of flame.

The horseless outlaws stood there, eyes stinging in the smoke that blurred their vision, guns dangling down at their sides. Then they floundered into the stream to escape the raging fire.

'Flim-flammed!' Keel panted again, kicking futilely at the water.'God-*damnittohell!*'

CHAPTER 8

CLOSED RANGE

Trent couldn't believe it when he saw who his rescuer was, although at just about the same time he realized the smoke smelled differently to gunpowder smoke and had the more sulphurous tang of fireworks.

'Sorry I got held up,' Clinton Gage told him way back in a clearing that was beyond the reach of the blazing brush. They could see the surviving outlaws floundering in the stream, getting as far from the flames as possible. 'I arrived at the jail just as Tag Benedict rode out with you. At the same time, two of the young lads I'd left to handle the fireworks ran up and said some of the fuses had pulled loose – I'd planned to use the fireworks as a diversion for when I broke you out of jail but Benedict beat me to that and I had to tend to those fuses so as not to disappoint the crowds anyway.'

Trent, dazed and feeling like the survivor of a train crash, shook his head slowly as Gage brought a saddled horse out of the brush, the one he had used to carry his fireworks up here. 'You were gonna bust me out of jail?'

'Yes, it was my fault you were there, even if I didn't have control when I was under the anaesthetic and, as you'd pointed out, you did save my life a year ago.'

'We-ell, it was kind of accidental. I really thought you were dyin' when I left you.'

'We can talk later. We'd best get out of here. They won't catch their horses before morning, maybe not till later in the day. But from what I know of Benedict and Keel they won't take this lying down.'

Gage led the way through the dark timber, climbing the range. Looking back, Trent, still light-headed, saw the brushfire was dying down now.

'You fooled me. I thought it was an attack by a posse.'

Gage nodded. 'Took me hours to set up and get the fuses just right. Couple of them didn't burn, or there'd have been even more noise and smoke. I watched them beat you. I'm sorry, Trent. I'm no hero and not much with a gun.'

Trent smiled thinly. 'You did all right. I take it back, that crack about you bein' a greenhorn.'

'Well, maybe half a one, I'm still not what you'd call a true dyed-in-the-wool westerner.'

'Never could be unless you were born to it and even some of them don't make it. I'm obliged, Gage. If you ever figured you owed me somethin', you're all squared away now and then some.'

Gage nodded and moved ahead on his big chestnut with the jet-black tail and mane. Trent followed more slowly on his roan, feeling every small jolt through his aching body as they climbed higher and the air became colder. They camped amongst some boulders just over the crest and Gage lit a fire in a shallow trench he dug and screened it with other rocks. He smiled at the watching Trent. 'I remembered how you built that fire to heat your knife blade.'

'You're a queer one, Gage. I dunno quite what to make of you and ain't that the gospel truth.'

'Just take me as you find me.'

'Sounds fair.'

After three cups of strong, freshly brewed coffee, laced with a liberal dash of whiskey each time, and some cold beef and biscuits, Gage lit cheroots for them both, studied his battered companion and asked quietly, 'Just what were they trying to beat out of you?' As Trent snapped his head up, Gage added, 'They seemed very determined.'

'Mix up,' Trent said shortly. 'Tag thought I'd taken somethin' I shouldn't've from that Cricket Creek bank.'

'Something of his, I gather?'

'Somethin' he claimed was his, but I guess it belongs to anyone who can hang onto it now.'

'Intriguing! Would I be out of line to ask you to elaborate?'

Trent took a couple of deep drags on his cheroot, gulped the last of his coffee before answering. 'There was s'posed to be a bag of diamonds in the bank safe,' he said and told Gage the story.

Gage smoked silently while he talked and remained silent for a few minutes after Trent had finished. 'And you didn't even know about the diamonds before the robbery?'

'None of us did except Tag and Chuck Keel.'

'Then it was just accidental you scooping up the satchel?'

'Sure. And in my hurry to get the buffalo stampedin' I left it and two bags of coins in my saddlebags. My horse went down under the buffs' hoofs. Trampled flat, I guess. I never hung round to find out.'

'So the satchel and coins would've been trampled into the ground? I mean into as in *under.*'

Trent nodded. 'Why so interested?'

'Twenty-five thousand dollars worth of diamonds there for the taking would interest almost anybody, wouldn't it?'

'Guess so, but you look more than just casually interested.'

Again Gage remained silent and the night sounds intruded: crickets, a mournful cry of some bird, a rush of unseen wings, a slithering in the rocks, the occasional crackle of the dying fire. 'I think Benedict might just go on to Horsehead Pass instead of chasing you right away, Trent.'

'And you.'

'Of course, he'll know it was me as soon as he realizes it was fireworks and not real guns, but my impression of Tag Benedict is that he'll put greed above all else. He'll go and check that stampede site for the satchel. If he doesn't find it, *then* he'll come after you, with renewed energy.'

'I aim to be a long way from here and some place he can't find me by that time.'

Gage stubbed out his cheroot, looking at Trent all the time. 'Money means nothing to you?'

'It means plenty to me, 'specially when I don't have

any. Like now.'

'Then why don't you go after the diamonds?'

Trent seemed uneasy. 'Because I reckon they won't be there. Sure they might be, but if they were just lyin' there in the dirt, someone over the last year using that pass could've found them.'

'And if they were trampled well into the ground, out of sight. . . ?'

Trent spread his arms. 'You'd have to dig up a couple of square miles, that's how much of the plains the buffalo stampeded over before they hit the pass and I lost sight of the grey long before then.'

'Wouldn't it be worth it? All the digging, I mean.'

Fargo Trent frowned now as he looked steadily at the other man. 'Gage, thanks to you, I'm still free but I still have a wanted dodger and a price on my head. I don't aim to hang around country where Dub Bracemore could turn up just on the chance of findin' diamonds I'm not even sure exist.'

Gage started to say something but seemed to catch himself, closed his mouth and shrugged. After a while, when they were rolling up in their blankets, shivering a little, he said, 'You're truly trying to go straight, aren't you, Trent?'

'Mostly it's tryin' to stay outta jail. I figure I've got more chance of doin' that if I'm law-abidin'. It ain't easy, but yeah, I am tryin'.'

'Then I wish you luck. You said earlier that I've more than "squared away" as you put it, anything I thought I owed you. Well, if that's so, can I ask you a favour? To kind of bring things to even-Steven?'

'What's that?'

'I owe you nothing; you owe me nothing. We get all squared away, no debts between us.'

Trent frowned again, finally nodded. 'Sure, I don't mind doin' you a favour if you need it. What is it?'

'Take me back to Horsehead Pass and show me where you believe the diamonds were lost.'

The three surviving outlaws were exhausted by the time they had rounded-up the horses and salvaged most of their riding gear. Some of the saddles had been burned and two bedrolls were now useless. The grub sack had suffered but some hardtack was edible if a man washed it down quickly with stream water.

Sitting dejectedly on the sand-bar across the stream, chomping with aching jaws on the smoke-smelling grub, they looked dirty and depressed and ready to give up.

Till Big Tom said, 'I guess we weren't no way meant to have them diamonds, boys.'

Both Keel and Benedict snapped their heads up, the latter with tufts of hair burnt off, reddened patches of scalp visible, a blister on one side of his face. Keel's hands were burned, too, and black with charcoal and dried blood. Big Tom was no better off, his clothing full of singed holes and his sideburns no more than black stubble now.

'Them diamonds are ours!' growled Tag Benedict. 'Don't think we're givin' up.'

'Hell, Tag, Fargo's got that fireworks man on his side now and we'll have Quinnell comin' after us when he figures it had to be you busted Fargo out!'

'Tom, you're just shook up some by that fire. We

know you was nearly burned to a crisp in that Yankee barn at Marlow Crossin'. But you survived that and you've survived this; we all have.' Tag looked at Keel as well as Big Tom Santos. 'We still dunno for sure where them stones are. Gage ain't much more'n a greenhorn. Trent's ten times tough as him, so Gage is no account.'

Keel stiffened. 'What the hell're you sayin'?'

'I'm sayin' we go after 'em! They might figure we'll head for Horsehead Pass, but I ain't convinced Trent ain't got them diamonds stashed away somewhere else. So we go get him and this fireworks son of a bitch and this time he'll talk or die!'

'That part I like,' Keel allowed. 'But if Fargo's got time to be ready for us. . . . He's hell in a handbasket, Tag, when he gets riled and he sure won't love us for roughin' him up.'

'We go after him. *Make* him talk. If he don't or if he dies before we get through with him, then we go to Horsehead Pass, but I gotta know first if he's coverin' up and got the stones cached someplace.' He stood and looked coldly at both men. 'Anyone don't want to come, then you're out now. And you stay out!'

Big Tom got lazily to his feet, hitching up his gunbelt. 'Well, I ain't gonna pass on this. If it takes a long ways round to get there, that's fine with me, long as we make it in the end.'

Benedict nodded, flicked his eyes to Keel. 'Chuck?'

Keel shrugged. 'Just promise me first lick at Trent and I'm in.'

'He's all yours,' Tag said happily, tugging at the singed ends of his moustache. 'Now let's see if we can pick up his trail.'

103

Gage surprised Trent with how well he knew this open range country. Twice he had insisted they veer away from the main trail and cut through tall timber because, he said, firstly, Indians had moved their summer camp more into the timbered hills this year because they had been hassled by new settlers moving in to their old campsites and, secondly, the way Trent intended to go led to a pass whose walls had collapsed after last winter's torrential rain.

'Not sure you need me to take you to Horsehead, Gage,' Trent opined as they edged out of the tall timber.

'I've been through here several times during the last year,' Gage said by way of explanation. 'Less and less open range now. Cattlemen are moving in. Best if we stay out of sight.'

The main thing now was to get back on the trail Trent had in mind, for the diversions had meant a considerable detour that took them over a low range. They paused on the crest, leaning on their saddlehorns, looking across a large valley where cattle dotted the slopes and rich green pastures.

'Didn't know land this far out had been settled,' Fargo Trent admitted.

'Was part of the old Indian lands but luckily they're a peaceful tribe and their numbers are dwindling. For a consideration of several hundred ponies and food, they moved camp a little way off from the original site.'

'Bet they had a lot of choice in that!'

Gage shrugged and led the way down the slope of

the mountain. Trent followed slowly, still stiff and sore. Gage had given him a rifle and sixgun and he watched the backtrail closely: he knew Tag might easily come after them first before going to look for the diamonds.

But it wasn't the backtrail where the new danger came from. It was ahead, when they picked their way carefully down the steepest part of a slope and came out through a boulder field onto the rim of a small canyon where cattle grazed around a distant waterhole.

The shot made Trent jump and he had his rifle half out of its scabbard when a voice warned curtly, 'Forget the guns or you're both dead men! Lift your hands, empty now! All right, stay that way.'

They could hear the horse pushing through the brush and Trent knew already by the voice to expect a woman. But never such a woman as appeared at the edge of the brush.

He had detected a slight accent in her warning words and now saw she was Mexican, or had a good deal of Spanish blood in her. Her skin was golden brown, hair glinting like a raven's wing in the light of sundown. She seemed tall in the saddle for a woman although, later, he found she came barely an inch above his shoulder. Clear dark brown eyes regarded Gage and Trent and gloved hands held a smoking Winchester carbine. Trent figured she would be in her mid-twenties or a little younger. The pale blouse bulged enough to be sure of her gender, but not exceptionally so. The hips in dark corduroy looked slender and exciting.

'You are trespassing,' she said in her warm voice, although there was no welcome in her face. The carbine's barrel settled between them, could be flicked either way if they tried to jump her.

'Didn't realize it, ma'am,' Trent said. 'More'n a year since I've been over this way.'

She gave him the once over then moved her gaze to Clinton Gage. 'This one has been here more recently. You came to my ranch house, offered to buy a meal and supplies.'

Gage nodded, smiling thinly. 'I recollect you seemed offended. Said money was not the question: I could eat and take a grubsack with me when I left but it was customary to offer to do some small job by way of appreciation. Not offer money.'

'Yes and you told me you knew nothing about ranch work and didn't know what you could offer to do.'

Trent glanced at Gage sharply. 'In your greenhorn days, huh?'

'I was just trying to be honest.'

'Wonder you didn't get shot or kicked out with an empty belly.'

'Mr Gage tried his best to explain,' the woman said curtly. 'I believed him. He had a certain inexperienced look.'

'Must have more charm than I figured.'

'I'd go along with that,' Gage said with a half-smile. 'Fargo, meet Señorita Isabella Vargas. Mistress of that ranch you see on the rise there. The *Rosalita* is the brand name if memory serves me correctly.'

Trent had never heard of it but he touched a hand to the battered hat and said mildly, '*Buenos días, señorita.* Fargo Trent at your service.'

'I think not, *señor.* You are still a trespasser.'

'We skirted the Indian camp and came a little too far

south before turning north again,' Gage explained. 'We mean you no harm.'

She laughed, briefly, without mirth, flicked the carbine's barrel. 'Of that I am certain! At the moment.'

'Just on our way through to Horsehead Pass,' Trent said quietly.

She frowned slightly. 'That is a hard ride from here. And it leads to a troubled trail.'

Gage frowned. 'It takes you to Cricket Creek eventually, doesn't it?'

'Eventually, if you are lucky. There are bandits and trail wolves of the two-legged kind.'

Gage and Trent exchanged glances, the latter saying, 'Doesn't sound like the place it was a year ago. Dub Bracemore kept the lawless element well down.'

Her eyes flashed. 'Yes, but Bracemore has not been sheriff for more than six months. He retired, because of ill health, I believe. A man named Griggs, his deputy, took over the sheriff's job but although he considers himself a hard man, he is not much of a lawman.'

'He's no kind now,' Trent said, adding when he saw her puzzled face, 'He's dead. Ambushed up north by a man named Tag Benedict.'

'That outlaw!' she breathed. 'He is a wanted man. So, Asa Griggs is dead. I wonder now what will happen along that trail through the pass?'

'You had trouble, *señorita?*' Trent asked, and she nodded.

'*Sí*, much trouble. We used to drive our herds through to the railhead at Cricket Creek. Bad men have made it impossible for us to go that way now. If they don't steal our cows, they hold us to ransom for safe passage. We have to skirt the mountain range and drive all the way to Century.'

'Mighty long way round!' allowed Trent.

Gage agreed, but it was clear he had something else on his mind other than the troubled trail through Horsehead Pass. 'You said Sheriff Bracemore retired?'

'Yes. Ill health was the reason he gave.'

'Uh-huh.' Gage paused and caught Trent's eye. The outlaw frowned, not reading Gage's look. The man addressed the woman again. 'You happen to know where Sheriff Bracemore is now, *señorita?*'

She seemed surprised at the man's interest but nodded slowly. 'Yes, he bought a large ranch at the other end of this valley.' She gestured vaguely with her whip. 'The Fallen T, one of the most prosperous in the Territory but the owner died suddenly and the family put it up for sale.'

Gage's eyes were penetrating now, his shoulders slumped as he said to Trent, 'I think we can save ourselves a ride, Fargo. No point in going to Horsehead Pass now. I think it's pretty clear that the satchel has already been found. What d'you say?'

CHAPTER 9

DEAD MEN CAN'T QUIT

Trent felt a whole lot better after the cuts and bruises had been washed and disinfected and arnica rubbed in gently. Bandages supported his bruised ribs. The small but deep cut above his left eye had been expertly stitched with catgut by the gentle fingers of Isabella Vargas.

'I'm mighty obliged for all this, *señorita*,' Trent said as she set a cup of strong coffee before him, floated a good spoonful of brandy onto the steaming surface.

'It is inherited, I think: my father was a doctor.'

She was standing in the sunlight filtering through the leaves of a willow that shaded the table where he sat. It was on a flagstoned patio attached to the ranch house and she took a seat opposite him, a glass of lemonade beside her hand. Her dark eyes studied him.

'I have seen your face before, Mr Trent. I'm not sure I remember where, but I think it may have been on the

109

wall outside the post office in Century.' Suddenly she smiled. 'Please don't look so alarmed! I pride myself on being a good judge of men, just as I decided Clinton Gage was mostly new to the ways of the frontier, but meant well.'

Trent fiddled with the coffee cup, turning it round and round in its saucer by the handle. 'You won't mind if I don't comment.'

Her smile came back. She shook her head. 'No, I will not mind!' She gave a small laugh. 'I did not read what was beneath your picture on the poster. It was your face that interested me, not your deeds.'

He sipped some of the coffee, almost jumped out of the chair when it scalded his mouth but somehow managed to swallow and look reasonably calm when what he really wanted to do was curse and run across the ranch yard for a gallon of cold well-water.

'Why did you bring Gage and me back here?' he asked flatly.

She flicked up one dark, curving eyebrow. 'You obviously needed attention for your hurts.'

He waited for more but that, apparently, was her explanation in full. He sighed. 'Well, I can only say again that I'm mighty obliged to you. I'll be on my way after I finish this coffee.'

'Mr Gage will be back soon and I have given orders for lunch to be served within the hour, Mr Trent. You would not refuse, surely?'

Trent frowned. 'Call me Fargo, or Trent, none of this "Mister". No, I won't pass up a decent lunch but I have to tell you, *señorita*. . . .'

'Bella, please.'

'OK,' I have to tell you, Bella, that if I'm found here, obviously having been tended by you . . .' He held up his iodine-dabbed hands and let his worn shirt gape to display the bandages about his torso. 'You'll be in a heap of trouble. I'm wanted for. . . .'

'Many things, I am sure,' she interrupted. 'Too many to be specific, I would think?'

His eyes watched her face and then he nodded slowly. 'You're right, less you know the better, but I have to at least tell you that there's a bounty on me.'

'One thousand dollars, yes, I remember that from the poster, but it does not interest me.' She waved her slim hands like a pair of flitting butterflies. 'As you can see, I am not poor. Anyone can always use extra money, of course, but it would matter to me where that money came from and how it was obtained.'

Trent took refuge in the coffee again, holding the cup in front of his face now: it was slightly cooler and he sipped carefully and frequently. There was a strange stirring within him and it took him a little time to realize it was caused by this stunning woman. *Hell, he had only just met her and yet he felt . . . What did he feel for her? Something alien to him. Something warm and caring . . . He could not recall any other woman he had ever felt this way about, except maybe his mother and two sisters. . . .*

Trent stopped the line of thought so suddenly that he almost choked on a mouthful of coffee. After the coughing and spluttering was over, he took the cloth she handed him and wiped his face and shirt-front. He felt his ears hot, knew they looked scarlet. *He was making a damn fool of himself!*

'Why don't you rest here in the shade, relax, *amigo*

mio. You will be called when lunch is ready and we can talk over good food and perhaps a bottle of wine from my father's estate in Durango, eh?'

He watched her go back into the house, frowning, sweating, although a cooling breeze caressed his face as the willows stirred. All of these feelings were so damn new and unexpectedly strange.

He wished she had left the brandy bottle on the table.

A shadow falling across his face made him sit up hurriedly and he opened his eyes, aware hazily that he must have dozed off. Against the midday sun he saw a tall silhouette that he knew was not Isabella Vargas. He edged his hand towards the butt of the sixgun holstered on his right hip.

'Take it easy, Trent,' said Gage, thrusting out a hand towards him. 'Isabella says to come in to lunch whenever you're ready.'

'Fine.' Trent straightened in the chair. 'Where've you been?'

'Took a quick ride up-valley and had a look at that Fallen T spread. Fargo, it's like a damn empire! No way in hell could someone like Dub Bracemore, a local sheriff, ever pay for something like that out of his monthly wage!'

'So you reckon it more or less confirms he found the satchel of diamonds?'

'Has to! Either that or he dug up a nugget of gold from beside his outhouse and then pushed the outhouse into the hole to fill it in.'

Trent smiled. 'You're startin' to sound like a genuine westerner, Clinton, *amigo!*'

112

'I'll take that as a compliment.' Gage sounded genuinely pleased. But he was sobering some now, mouth taking on a tight stretch. 'I'm no expert, but I reckon you'd need every single one of twenty-five thousand dollars worth of diamonds to pay for that ranch. A massive house, half a dozen outbuildings, any of which a family of settlers would give their eye-teeth for. Horses with excellent lines, and I do happen to know a little about horses, and cattle scattered for miles in lush pastures.'

Trent frowned. 'Sounds like old Dub got himself a real bargain.'

Gage shook his head emphatically. 'Dub didn't strike me as a man bright enough to talk himself a good deal.'

'Well, what're you thinkin'?'

'I'm thinking we ought to go find out just what's been going on.'

Trent was already shaking his head before Gage was finished speaking. 'Count me out. I'm not goin' near any lawman, retired or not. Listen, I don't care if he found the diamonds and used 'em to buy the Fallen T or anythin' else. I just want to get outta this neck of the woods and start over. I guess I'll make for the north, Yankee country, which I don't care for, but it's a long way from here.'

'And Isabella,' Gage pointed out with a slow smile. 'Oh, don't look like that, Trent! I saw right away how you two hit it off. Neither of you realized it, I'm sure, but it's one of those things the dime novel romances do so well: love at first sight.'

Trent lurched to his feet, not smiling. In fact, he looked more shocked than anything. 'To hell with you,

113

Gage! You're talkin' through your hat. I'm hungry. I'm goin' in for lunch.'

And he strode towards the house, buttoning his shirt. Gage continued to smile faintly, shook his head and hurried after him.

He didn't aim to let Trent get away that easily.

Dub Bracemore might have been a bumbling lawman and none too bright in other ways, but he wasn't a man who cut corners where his personal safety was concerned.

And Gage and Trent were just a little bit too confident that they would be able to find a quiet, safe place where they could watch the goings-on at Fallen T through field glasses.

They found the place all right, a perfect spot for what they had in mind. Shaded by trees, on the side of the hill that caught the afternoon breeze, and with chest-high brush and a line of man-sized boulders that gave both men and mounts cover.

They had been watching the cowboys below go about their ranch duties for over an hour and Trent was growing irritable. His ribs were aching from lying stretched out for so long and there was nothing untoward to see, anyway. The cowboys were being cowboys: branding calves and a few rough mavericks, shoeing a brace of horses, curry-combing others and, in a smaller pen, a man was breaking-in a mount fresh from the brush. It was giving him hell, throwing him within seconds of mounting each time. But he stubbornly got to his feet, dusted himself off and climbed back into the saddle again to go sailing through the air over the horse's head almost as soon as he'd settled.

Gage, who had the glasses now, chuckled. 'That ranny's going to be black and blue by supper-time if he keeps fighting that mustang!'

'Yeah, he's bein' stubborn, not smart: he ought to take time to out-think that jughead.' Trent started to ease back to get to his feet. 'But I don't aim to stick around and see any more, Gage. It's plain enough, Bracemore found the satchel and bought himself a decent retirement. If it keeps him off my neck, I don't give a damn. I never want to see him again.'

'But he'll want to see you!'

Trent turned swiftly, hand streaking to his gun-butt. He froze when he saw the tall man in checkered shirt and grey corduroy trousers standing beside a boulder, covering him and Gage with a cocked Winchester.

'Lift 'em easy, gents, then start walkin' down the slope to the ranch house. Sounds to me like Sheriff Dub'll be mighty glad to see you two.'

'Thought this was his retirement?' Trent said, but obeying and lifting his hands. Gage followed his example.

'Whatever it is, it's Dub's private business. I'm hired to see no one comes along to bother him. Might've heard of me, name's Daniels. They call me "Danny Doom".'

Gage sucked in a sharp breath but Trent's expression didn't change, except his eyes narrowed a little.

'You come a long way down the ladder since ridin' sidekick to Cap'n Quantrill, Doom.'

The newcomer's face was instantly alert and he peered more closely at Trent. After a time he nodded slowly. 'Fargo Trent. Yeah, you were one of the yeller-bellies quit the Cap'n, ran home with your tail between your legs.'

'Just got tired of all the butchery, Doom. Kept the Good Fight goin' my own way till it became a way of life . . . Till I met up with Tag.' Trent sounded a bit wistful here, unaware of it. 'Hard times and hard to shake off but I aim to do it.'

Danny Doom snorted. 'You! Trent, you're a dyed-in-the-wool outlaw! You'll never quit the owlhoot!'

'Givin' it a try. You drag me in to face Bracemore and I reckon I'll end up in jail instead of quittin'.'

'Dead men can't quit, Trent!'

Fargo stiffened at the unexpected remark and Gage licked his lips. Then Doom gestured with the rifle and marched them through the brush and down into the ranch yard. Another rider they hadn't noticed up on the ledge led their mounts down behind them.

Dub Bracemore was sitting on a large porch at a table, chewing the end of a pencil as he sweated over a thick ledger, others scattered around. A crumpled, blood-spotted kerchief lay atop them. He glanced up then straightened quickly in his cane chair, tossing the well chewed pencil onto the table amongst the paper and books. Gage and Trent were shocked at how he had changed in just over a year. Thinner, hollow-eyed, sallow and coughing: a dead man walking.

'Well, damn me if this ain't a surprise! *Two* Fargo Trents!' Dub wiped the kerchief across his mouth and chuckled at their puzzlement, pointed to Gage. 'You turned out to be the wrong'n, but that there feller beside you is the real thing. Am I right, Trent?'

'You're not a lawman any longer, Dub.'

'What was that you fellers used to say? Once a lawman, always a lawman?'

Trent shook his head. 'What we used to say, Dub, was, "Once a lawman, never a man".'

Bracemore's face straightened and he sucked down another breath: it looked a painful process. Doom was ready when Bracemore nodded and he swung the rifle barrel at Trent's head.

But Trent was ready too, ducked, reached out with his left hand and wrenched the rifle barrel to one side, then hit the gunman in the midriff with a solid blow. Doom gagged and doubled up, releasing his hold on the Winchester. Trent reversed it and slammed the butt against the man's head. Danny Doom sprawled on his face in the gravel and Trent put the rifle on the ranny who had brought in the horses.

'Just leave the reins trail, feller, then go find yourself some chore to do.'

The man didn't have to be told twice and as he hurried off Trent faced Dub Bracemore squarely. The ex-lawman was holding his kerchief to his mouth again and his voice was muffled between coughs, chest heaving. He licked his lips under the tobacco-yellow frontier moustache. 'I ain't armed. Don't carry a gun nowadays.'

'Well, it's a mistake if you were relyin' on Danny-boy for protection,' Trent said. 'What were you gonna do, Dub? Kill me and claim the bounty?'

Bracemore didn't have to reply: his guilty look answered for him. Trent shook his head slowly as Gage glanced around him nervously, but so far the cowboys way down by the corrals were carrying on with their chores. The ranny Trent had sent away would soon spread the word there was trouble up at the house, though.

'Looks like your claim to have to retire early was genuine, Dub,' Trent allowed and the ex-lawman glared over the kerchief, lowered it slowly, scowling.

'You think it ain't, I'll cough all over you, then all you gotta do is wait!'

'Dub, we know you found that satchel of diamonds,' Gage said suddenly and Trent frowned a little: seemed to him that Gage had one hell of an interest in those stones. 'And you bought this place with them.'

Bracemore met Gage's gaze, his mouth pursed thoughtfully, still breathing hard with the lung fever. Then he gave a false smile, spread his hands out from his body. 'You ain't gonna blame a poor, underpaid, ailin' lawman for givin' way to temptation, are you? I mean, I been poorly for years, but carried on doin' my job just the same, hidin' my pain and troubles, just carryin' on because I'd took the Oath of Office.'

'*Law* office, Dub,' Gage said tightly. 'By keeping those diamonds you broke that oath. Now you're no different to any of the law-breakers you've chased over the years.'

'Chased and brought to justice!' Dub was quick to add, wheezing, hands clenched weakly into fists now. But he fought down his rising anger, realizing he had no brass star to back him in this and earn him his own way. His bony shoulders slumped. 'Look, fellers, I ain't the only law-breaker here, you both know that. Hell, I never hurt no one by keepin' that satchel. No one was around. I played a hunch and looked where them buffalo had stampeded, finally located the satchel, a strap buckle caught the sunlight and led me to it. When I seen them stones a-glintin' like a handful of stars, well. . . .' He shook his head slowly, fever bright eyes a mite dreamy. 'I swear I'd never seen nothin' like it an' somethin' happened to me. I thought, "Why not keep these? No one'll know and I can retire in about six months an' not have to worry about some measly pension to see me through what's left of my life?" ' His smile widened. 'I'd always dreamed of ownin' my own place, big an' peaceful and prosperous, just like this.' He gestured limply towards the spread of range. 'What would you fellers've done? Oh, I *know* what you'd've done, Trent: you'd already stole the stones in the first place. But you, Gage, you'd have been tempted too, wouldn't you? C'mon now, tell me the gospel truth!'

Clinton Gage nodded slowly. 'Yes, Dub, I'd've been tempted to do exactly what you did.'

Bracemore's smile now was almost ear-to-ear. 'Told you! Well, I'm sorry, gents, but there ain't nothin' left to share with you. This spread took every last cent.'

'What about the sacks of coins that were with the satchel?' asked Trent, his words wiping the smile from Bracemore's face. 'Don't play dumb! If you found the satchel, you had to've found the coins too, mostly gold, I believe.'

Dub took his time, finally nodded, releasing a long wheezy breath. Danny Doom started to stir but Trent casually hit him again with the rifle butt and he subsided. Dub's eyes pinched down.

'OK. There was some cash money, more silver then gold, I swear. Toted up to about two thousand and some odd bucks. It went to settin' up the spread. An' I took a trip to Denver to see a doctor.' He shook his head sadly. 'Weren't no good. I'm too far gone. Best I can do now is sit it out and enjoy for a little while what I've wanted for years. I swear that's gospel.'

'I believe it,' Trent said, but watching Gage curiously he asked quietly, 'You'd've really kept those stones?'

Gage was sober-faced. 'I said I'd've been *tempted* to keep them just like Bracemore here. No, I'd've kept the diamonds only long enough to return them to their rightful owners.' He paused, seeing the open scepticism on Bracemore's face, a milder version on Trent's. 'The same people who hired me to recover them.'

CHAPTER 10

WHITE LIE

Leaving the Fallen T spread, they paused once more on the ledge they had used to observe the ranch earlier. Trent's gaze was sharp and slow-moving as he watched their backtrail.

Gage noticed and tensed some. 'What is it? Someone coming after us?'

'Not yet.'

'What's that mean?' Gage asked, alarmed.

'Danny Doom, mean son of a bitch. He won't take that gunwhipping and Bracemore won't be able to hold him back even if he wants to.'

Gage ran a tongue over his lips, one hand on the leather case that carried the field glasses.

'Don't bother,' Trent said. 'You won't see Danny Doom. Might hear the shot that hits you in the middle of the back, then again you might just die between heart-beats without knowin' what the hell happened.'

'By God! You're a Job's comforter, Trent!'

Fargo smiled thinly. 'Just tellin' it like it is, Gage. Not like some folk I know.'

It was Gage's turn to smile crookedly. 'I see. Well, it's simple enough, Fargo. Trans-Continent, as you know, is a very rich and powerful organization and has many contacts. Some overseas. One company was the Veldt Mining Company of South Africa. They hired us to survey for copper and other minerals and arrange the construction of mineheads and so on. Also, some important documents were taken by mistake in a train hold-up and I was asked to locate them, negotiate their return.'

Trent nodded as Gage straightened in the saddle. 'You did your usual good job, so when their diamonds were stolen they asked you to go find 'em again.'

Clinton Gage looked a little put out that Trent had figured it out so quickly. 'Yes. T-C had fired me by then because of that run-in with Bracemore when he mistook me for you. The Dutchies didn't know that and I didn't tell them. They contacted me direct and offered me ten per cent of the diamonds' value if I could recover them. I needed the money and felt if I tracked you down I'd be well on the way to finding the stones, seeing as you were one of the gang who robbed the Cricket Creek bank. Well, it took a lot longer than anyone expected, but I'm still eligible for that percentage whenever I turn up the diamonds.'

Trent thought about it before saying, 'Then how come you left Bracemore where he was? I thought you'd at least take him and hand him over to the law.'

'To what purpose? He's a dying man. The diamonds have been spent, exchanged for the Fallen T. The only way the South Africans can possibly get their money back now is for Dub to sell up and hand the proceeds over.'

'You wait for that to happen and hell'd be froze over! Or maybe Dub'll die and who knows what'll happen to Fallen T then? He could have kinfolk.'

Gage nodded. 'Yes, there's nothing I can do to force him to sell up and repay the money. So I'll just send in my report and leave the Dutchies to decide whether to put pressure on Bracemore if that's what they want. If they do they'll hire the best legal men in the country.'

'And your conscience'll be clear and you hope to collect your ten per cent off the top.'

Gage was embarrassed. 'I've depended on getting that money for a long time, Fargo. They're honourable men. They'll hold to their deal.'

'That's not what I meant.' Trent stared hard at the other man. 'You still got a lot of greenhorn in you, Gage.'

'Not necessarily. I know the right thing to do, that's all.' He was working hard to sound convincing.

'It's a long way to South Africa from here. Dub could be dead before you even notify these Dutchmen.'

'Nevertheless, it *is* the right thing to do, Fargo, and I *intend* to do it. And, yes, I expect to receive my just reward too!'

Trent almost smiled at the belligerent look on Gage's face. He lifted his hands off the reins and made several pushing motions towards the other. 'OK, OK, don't get tough with me, pardner! I believe you. Just hope you can sleep well. Old Dub's right, you know. He's punched law on the frontier for most of his life. He's got nothin' out of it but a lot of scars and a fatal dose of lung-fever. He's tolerably happy now and he hasn't hurt anyone who'll feel the loss by keepin' those diamonds.'

'He broke the Law he swore to uphold!' Gage said stiffly and without another word, lifted his reins and started his chestnut across the ledge. Trent heeled his roan forward to follow, thinking, *smug, self-righteous bastard!*

The rifle cracked from the ridge above and Gage's horse's rear legs sagged violently, its rump swerving, unseating the rider. Gage went one way, the chestnut the other, dark mane and tail streaming as it ran into the brush behind sheltering boulders in a stumbling, weaving motion.

The gun fired twice more, kicking dust around Gage's rolling body and then turned towards Trent who was already wheeling the roan behind some rocks. Dust sprayed and the lead howled away in ricochet. Trent dismounted before the horse had slid to a stop, his Winchester in his hand as he flopped on his belly between two rocks that had a bush growing between them. Another dry-gulcher's bullet ripped leaves and twigs from the bush above Trent, sprinkling his shoulders as he settled. He had wrenched his aching ribs getting into position, grimaced as he worked the lever, eyes raking the slope above for gunsmoke.

There was an afternoon breeze but it wasn't very

strong and the pall of powder-smoke hadn't carried far. Trent, long used to such things, easily calculated the direction and distance. Even as he brought the rifle into line he saw the black streak of the rifle barrel up there and an instant later flame stabbed from its muzzle.

Trent instinctively ducked and the lead whined off the rock above him in a long spurting line, leaving a silver streak on the boulder that would soon dull and fade. Trent came up, cartridge already in the chamber, finger curling on the trigger. The butt settled firmly into his shoulder, the blade foresight fell naturally in the V of the rear sight. The butt kicked and the lever clashed almost before the bullet had left the muzzle. The rifle bucked again and again, the lead raking the area Trent had figured the powder-smoke was coming from.

He heard the man curse from way down here and he smiled, calling, 'You never learned a damn thing from Cap'n Quantrill, did you, Danny? "Always kill the most dangerous lookin' ranny first." You should've nailed me, not Gage.'

His rifle fired twice more and he heard Doom slip and fall and then Trent was up and weaving his way upslope, doubled over. It hurt his ribs like hell and the breath blasted through his clenched teeth, but he made it and by the time Danny Doom had gotten back into position, Trent was only three yards away and coming in like a charging steer.

Doom looked up and his eyes flew wide. He dropped the rifle and palmed up his sixgun in a blur of speed but he was too late. Trent's rifle braced against his hip and lever and trigger emptied the magazine, the bullets hammering Danny Doom back and to one side. When his body rolled off the boulder, it left red smears across the sandstone.

Gage came in cautiously, his own gun in his hand but down at his side. Trent was already thumbing fresh loads into the rifle's tubular magazine.

'Gun ain't gonna do you no good danglin' like that.'

Gage looked at the weapon and rammed it back into his holster. His face was gravel-scarred from his fall, a sleeve of his shirt torn. He glanced at the bullet-riddled Danny Doom, asked, deadpan, 'Did you get him?'

Trent looked startled, snapped his head up, then smiled thinly. 'Hell, didn't know you had a sense of humour!'

'I thought you were never going to stop firing! And you were right about "dear old Bracemore" sending Doom after us.' Bitter sarcasm didn't sound quite right coming from Gage, somehow.

'Could be that Danny decided on his own to come, which is more likely. Though old Dub'd be happy if you were dead and buried: he knows you're dangerous to him now. Which is maybe why Doom shot at you first. He did know better and ought to've gotten me outta the way before worryin' about you.'

'The "greenhorn" you mean?' Gage sounded tense but stayed in control. 'Don't know that I can give Dub the benefit of the doubt, really.'

'Well, if I was you, I wouldn't think of goin' back. He'll have his crew backin' him this time.'

'So what do we do? Go back to Isabella's?'

Trent hesitated. 'You go if you want.'

'What? Where're you going?'

Trent waved an arm: *out there*. Gage frowned. 'You're afraid of Benedict?'

'Let's say I'd rather not tangle with him right now. Nor Quinnell, who'll be comin' too. There's a lot of country out there and now it's time for it to swallow me up. Likely the best chance I'll get.'

'Isabella will be disappointed.'

Gage smiled a little but Trent's face remained sober. 'She's better off without gallows bait like me.'

'She should be the one to decide that.'

'I'm decidin' it. Doom was from my past and there's more than him with scores to settle. Quinnell will show soon and he's Law. Tag's bound to come in some time soon too, and Bella can sure do without him in her life.'

Gage continued to keep his eyes firmly on Trent. 'Fargo, I'm sure you'll never admit this to yourself, but you're basically a decent man. I think Isabella knows this.'

'Sure, she can frame my picture after she cuts it out of a wanted dodger.'

'You're too hard on yourself. You're trying to make a . . . a decent, more honest life for yourself. I think you can get a damn good start with Isabella Vargas.'

'You're entitled to your opinion, Gage, but when we reach the fork in the trail, you'll be ridin' alone back to the Rosalita.'

He started back towards his mount, stopping while Gage caught up and they examined the wounded chestnut. It was only a bullet crease across the rump and in minutes they rode over the crest and down the slope to where the trail lay, one fork leading into the valley, the other to who knew where?

Gage slowed and hipped in the saddle. 'You know, Fargo, Tag Benedict could still show up at Rosalita. Those are only ordinary cowboys Isabella employs. She could probably do with some more protection. I mean, even if I stay for a while, I'm no gunfighter.'

Trent frowned, his mouth tight as he glared at Gage. Then he lifted his reins and his roan shouldered the chestnut aside as Trent put him up the trail leading to the valley. 'Damn you, Gage!'

Gage grinned and rode up alongside. 'See? You do have a conscience!'

'What I have is a strong urge to put a bullet into the first man I see on my right! If I turn that way!'

Gage's chuckle reached him and irritated him no end. 'I'm glad there's such fine scenery to look at on your left then, Fargo!'

Trent grunted. 'And I ain't sure I'm gonna let you tell these Dutchies about old Dub.'

That made Gage stiffen in the saddle. 'Now, look, that's up to me!'

'If I don't approve and I do nothin' about it, that makes me as bad as you.'

Gage hauled rein. 'Bad? As *bad* as me?'

'You're so damn busy wantin' to be seen to do what you figure is the "right thing" that you can't see when it's time to do the *decent* thing, whether it's right or wrong.'

Gage frowned: he didn't seem to have a ready answer to that.

But by the time they approached the Rosalita ranch, Fargo Trent had lost some of his anger that he had been using to brace him for his return to Isabella.

There had been women in his life, of course, but being on the run for all those years, they had been of fleeting interest and, truth to tell, he had never met one before who drew feelings from him like those he had for Isabella Vargas. He was uncomfortable feeling this way but, at the same time, there was a warmth there he had never experienced before. He found she was in his thoughts almost all the time, even when he was riding into danger or had other problems that required his immediate attention.

At first the intrusion had made him mad, but he was honest enough to admit to himself that, basically, he *enjoyed* thinking about the Mexican woman. At any time. . . .

But now, when it came time to face up to her again, he wasn't sure that he could do it or even *should* do it.

The kind of life he led, and would be leading in the future, offered nothing to a woman of her breeding. He had an uneasy, stomach-wrenching feeling that she would stick by him no matter what, but how could he allow that? Take her from the secure and comfortable life she now led into the unknown, where old enemies might appear at any time, some wearing a lawman's star, others just with a cocked gun in their hands.

'Gage,' he said suddenly as the other started to put his weary, limping mount down the slope that led onto the outskirts of Rosalita's home pastures. 'Been nice knowin' you, specially when you set off all them fireworks at Tag Benedict's camp.'

129

Clinton Gage hipped in the saddle, frowning as he hauled rein. 'You've changed your mind about coming down to the ranch house?'

Trent barely nodded. 'Given it some thought ridin' in. Best this way.'

'Not for Isabella and certainly not for you. I mean it, Trent! I'm sure this woman can help you.'

'I'm just as sure I don't need her help. But, like I said, I'm obliged to you, Gage. Maybe we'll meet again.'

Gage put his mount in closer, studied the stubborn, iron-jawed face, then sighed and offered his right hand. 'I hope so, Fargo. I probably won't contact the Dutchmen, except to say the diamonds are lost forever, down a bottomless sinkhole or something: a white lie. I guess I was still miffed at Dub for the way he treated me. Time I grew up.'

'Well, you're learnin' pretty fast, Clint. You might even make a Westerner one day.'

Gage grinned from ear to ear. 'Coming from you, Fargo! Well, I guess I . . . I'm overwhelmed.'

Trent nodded as they gripped briefly and firmly. They were starting to turn their mounts in different directions when a voice said from the rocks on the rise behind them,

'Aw, now ain't that nice! Just a coupla of friends at the partin' of the ways!'

Trent knew the voice at once and started to wheel his mount back, right hand going for his sixgun.

'Don't do it, Trent! You're fast, but not fast enough to beat a fallin' gun hammer!'

Tag Benedict walked his mount out of the rocks and covered both men with his shotgun. He bared his teeth as Trent let his hand fall away from his Colt. Gage was already lifting his hands shoulder high.

'Grab a handful of sky, too, Fargo!' Tag snapped. 'Then head on down the slope to the house where that fine-lookin' Mex woman is busy entertainin' Chuck an' Big Tom, I reckon. Can't wait to get my share!'

CHAPTER 11

THE ROSALITA

When they rode slowly into the ranch yard, Trent stiffened in the saddle and his teeth clenched.

Two men were sprawled at their ease on the porch. He recognized them as Chuck Keel and Big Tom Santos.

His knuckles whitened as they tightened around the reins. 'If she's been hurt, Tag. . . !'

Benedict chuckled. 'What? What'll you do? What you think you'll be *able* to do, huh? C'mon, Fargo! You've seen it all before.'

Gage looked sharply at Trent as Tag spoke these words and the anger spreading across his face changed abruptly as Benedict added, ' 'Course you used to ride off down to the crick or somewheres while we had our fun, but you knew what was goin' on.'

'It better not have gone on here,' Trent said, cold eyes drilling into Benedict who showed signs of discomfort that quickly changed to anger.

'Get it through your head that you don't have a say

in *nothin'* right now, Fargo! You do as *I* say!' Tag raised the shotgun threateningly.

Trent's gaze never wavered. 'I'll kill you, Tag, and those two as well.' The threat was delivered quietly, not casually, but without much heat, just a flat statement. And Gage saw that it shook Benedict despite his curling lip.

Provocatively, he looked past Trent to the porch, calling, 'How was she, boys? Full of that good ol' Mexican fire? Scratchin' an' bitin' an'. . . .'

His voice trailed off as Chuck Keel stood up slowly and they all saw his arm was bandaged from wrist to armpit and there was a raw red gouge down one side of his face. Big Tom struggled upright in his chair and they saw the bloody ear and the torn shirt-front with claw marks visible on his throat, disappearing down into the folds of the cloth.

Gage whistled through his teeth. 'My, oh, my! Looks like your men tangled with a mountain lion, Benedict!'

'Shut up!' roared Tag, hefting the shotgun, still looking at his injured men. 'The hell happened. . . ?'

'She's got a knife,' Chuck Keel said a little reluctantly. 'Dunno where it come from but she'd like to cut my nuts off! Missed by a whisker and next thing she's ripped my arm open and missed my eye by a hair! She. . . .'

'You goddamn fools!' Tag was disgusted. 'Two hard-cases like you couldn't even handle a greaser woman!'

'She's a damn spitfire, Tag!' Big Tom said mournfully. 'Ruther tackle a full-growed black bear, I swear!'

Trent smiled and Gage looked mildly amused, until Benedict said in a steely voice, 'Climb down and keep your hands up. An' don't do nothin' else till I tell you!'

As they obeyed Trent asked, 'What happened to the cowhands?'

Benedict seemed as if he would ignore the question, then said, with a jerk of his head, 'Shut 'em in the bunkhouse an' barn. Threw their guns down the well.'

'You're goin' soft, Tag. I expected the usual slaughter.'

'Shut up, Fargo, if you know what's good for you!' Still sitting his horse, the shotgun ready for action, Tag stared past his sorry-looking wounded warriors to the house. 'You in there! *Señorita*! This is Tag Benedict. You've heard of me: I say I'm gonna kill someone or blow their arm off you know I'll do it!' He waited for a reply but there was no answer so he continued, cocking both hammers on the Greener and aiming it at Trent. 'From here, with the spread of double-ought buckshot, I reckon I can blow Trent's right leg clear across the yard to your well and that's what I'm gonna do if you don't come out here in ten seconds, no knife, nothing but your pretty dress or whatever you're wearin'. Now I know you heard and I ain't gonna repeat it. Count starts now. I ain't makin' it out loud, neither, so you won't know when I reach ten till the shotgun goes off and Trent's only got one boot to polish for the rest of his life, which won't be much, OK?'

His lips started moving silently and Trent watched, tensed, mouth dry. Gage's eyes were widening as the seconds passed and he said with a hoarse choking sound, 'Fargo!'

Trent was wondering if he could dive to one side, use the steps as some sort of cover, as Benedict lifted the shotgun to his shoulder and curled a finger round the first trigger. Then the door opened and their released collective breaths sounded like a snake den at mating time.

Isabella, hair dishevelled, blouse a little torn and dirty, stepped onto the porch. A slim *cuchillo* glinted in her hand and she flipped it with an easy, expert motion of her wrist so that the blade quivered in the porch post at the top of the stairs. Her black eyes glinted as she looked at Tag Benedict. 'You win this round, Benedict!' she said quietly.

'An' I'll win the next and all the others just as easy,' Tag said, lowering the gun's hammers and holding the weapon across his thighs. He ran his gaze over the woman and despite herself she blushed and moved uncomfortably. 'I'll bet any marks I have on me after I've finished with you will be love bites or claw marks where your fingernails've sunk into my back, *querida!*' He laughed briefly. 'Yeah, that worries you, don't it? You know you'll be dealin' with a *real* man when I get around to you.'

'Remember what I said, Tag,' Trent reminded him softly. His face was murderous and Gage was sure he saw Benedict actually blanche as he straightened abruptly in the saddle. He covered up by dismounting and Big Tom and Chuck Keel nudged each other as they looked at the girl.

'Tag sure has winnin' ways, don't he?' Big Tom said.

'Never heard a woman he was with complain yet.'

'That's 'cause they ain't usually in good enough shape to complain or anythin' else when Tag rides out!'

Gage glanced worriedly at Trent but the man was

standing easily, though his face was taut, his eyes like the tips of bullets, looking at Benedict.

'Sorry I couldn't get back any quicker, Bella,' he said to the woman and she gave him a brief smile.

'You are here now and I feel better.'

'Aw, ain't that pretty?' Benedict mocked. 'She feels better, *safer*, I guess she means, all because good ol' Fargo is Johnny-on-the-spot! Makes you kinda shivery and feel good all over, don't it?'

Keel and Big Tom grinned. This was the Tag they liked best: in command, arrogantly so, supremely confident that things were under his control, willing to exchange banter because he *knew* he was going to have his way whenever, wherever he pleased.

'Lady, now don't you move an inch. Chuck, you stand between her and the door. Big Tom, you keep an eye on Trent; the greenhorn don't count, but watch him just in case.'

Benedict moved up the stairs, shotgun once again covering Trent and Gage. At the top, he used one hand to pull the *cuchillo* out of the post, arched his eyebrows admiringly as he quickly examined the blade.

'Looks like one of them knives some of the Mex whores keep strapped to their thigh just in case some ranny cuts up rough.' He laughed suddenly, glanced at his men. 'Cuts up rough! Get it?'

They laughed dutifully but Tag sobered fast, placed the knife between Isabella's breasts. He flicked it and cut away some of her blouse, not enough to embarrass her, but the threat was there. He glanced at Trent.

'Just tell me where the satchel is, Fargo.'

Trent didn't speak right away but then asked, 'And if I do?'

'Best worry about if you don't,' Tag said, then shrugged. 'We'll go get it and when we have it, well hell, I guess you won't want to keep ridin' with the old bunch, Fargo, so you go your way and we'll go ours.'

Deadpan, Trent asked, 'What about Gage?'

Tag shrugged. 'Hell, he don't matter a hill of beans to me, one way or t'other. You take care of him or let him go his own way. Up to you.'

'And Bella?'

Tag smirked slyly. 'We-ell. . . .'

Trent knew the man was deliberately provoking him. 'Well, what?'

'Well, what the hell! You interested? OK, she's yours, but only after we have the satchel and what's in it. We don't find it or we find it and the stones ain't in it, well, we'll need to do some more negotiatin'. How's that for a deal?'

'Guess it's the best I'll get.'

'Trent! He won't . . .' began Gage who was sweating profusely now. But he broke off when Trent lifted a hand.

'I know Tag better'n you, Clint. I know what he will and won't do.'

'Then how can you listen to what he's saying?'

'Because, like I said, it's the best deal I can hope for; *all of us can hope for.*'

Gage looked kind of sick and the girl, though pale, held the front of her torn blouse but remained silent, her eyes on Trent all the time.

Benedict grinned. 'Now you're showin' some of that

there good sense you is famous for, Fargo! So where's the satchel?'

'Thought I told you back in Drumhead jail.'

Benedict was growing impatient. 'You told me diddily-squat! Gave me some hogwash about it havin' been trampled into the ground when you stampeded a herd of buffalo, like you was stallin' me, just sayin' somethin' to keep me happy. An' its sounds like you're stallin' me *now*!'

Trent shrugged. 'You should've looked into my eyes, Tag. I told you the truth.'

Tag Benedict looked mighty unhappy now and the Greener lifted slightly. Chuck Keel and Big Tom held their breaths, waiting for the thunder of the weapon.

'It *is* the truth!' Gage said quickly and shivered slightly when Tag's gaze turned in his direction. 'He told me the same thing, explained how he'd panicked when he saw the posse drawing close and in his rush forgot to take his saddlebags off his horse and the satchel was in those bags with some coins. Give him the benefit of the doubt, Tag!'

Tag glanced at him, then leaned the shotgun against the wall, straightening as if he was taking a kink out of his back. Suddenly there was a sixgun blazing in his right hand and Isabella gave a small cry, her hands covering her mouth as the gunshot slapped at her ears and Gage reeled, staggering as he tried to keep balance but lost the short, desperate battle and collapsed on his side in the dirt.

Cowboys appeared in the doorways of the barn and the bunkhouse and Trent tensed but Tag smiled sardonically.

'No help there for you, Trent! They been told earlier,' and here he raised his voice, looking towards the ranch hands, 'that if they poke their noses outside the barn or the bunkhouse the woman loses a finger or worse! Ain't that right, boys?'

The men hurriedly backed-up into the buildings, closing the doors. By now Trent was kneeling beside Gage who was moaning and thrashing, his shirt-front red with blood.

'Seem to've done somethin' like this before,' Fargo said lightly, though he frowned at the blood pumping out of the wound which was high in Gage's shoulder. The bullet must have come so close to smashing the collarbone that it actually grazed it. Might be splinters of bone in there.

The woman was beside him now, pushing his hands aside as she examined the wound. Face pale and tight, eyes bright with anger, she told Benedict, 'He needs immediate attention or he'll bleed to death!'

Benedict shrugged. 'Get what you need and come back.'

'I can work on him best in the house.'

'You'll work on him where I say or not at all!' Benedict snapped, his face telling her plainly he was through pussyfooting around. He cocked the sixgun slowly.

Grim faced, she nodded and hurried into the house. Tag smiled crookedly at Trent. 'Gabby sort, ain't he? Well, mebbe that'll teach him to keep his mouth shut and mebbe it'll show you that I'm through listenin' to loco stories! When I ask where them stones are hidden, Fargo, I want straight talk or Gage is gonna have a few

139

more leaks to need pluggin'! Savvy?'

Trent, pressing Gage's weak hand over the necker-chief he had wadded over the wound, stood slowly.

'At the risk of you shootin' me, Tag, it was gospel what I said. If you're gonna find that satchel at all, it'll be out near Horsehead Pass where I stampeded the buffalo.'

The smoking Colt rose and the hammer notched back under Benedict's thumb. His eyes were narrowed and murderous.

'I warned you, damn it!'

'T . . . tell him . . . Fargo!' gritted Gage. 'For God's. . . !'

'Yeah, Fargo,' mocked Tag. '*Tell me, you son of a bitch!*'

Then Isabella came hurrying out of the house with a dish of hot water, rags and bottles clasped awkwardly or tucked under her arms. Trent ignored Tag and went to help her set the things out on a towel she laid beside Gage who looked like a corpse already, although his eyes were wide open.

It somehow broke the spell and Tag's face softened just a shade, even as the muzzle of the sixgun followed Trent's every move.

'Your story's easy enough to prove, ain't it? You just take us to this place near Horsehead Pass and we'll have a looksee for ourselves.' As Trent slowly nodded, Tag added viciously, ' 'Course the woman comes with us and I reckon Gage'll be able to make it there.' He chuckled. 'Notice I said there, nothin' about there an' back!'

'A ride like that will kill him!' protested the woman, aghast at the suggestion.

Benedict shrugged, keeping his gaze on Trent. 'Well,

that's a possibility, I guess. *You* could get yourself killed one way or another too, *querida*, ain't that so, Fargo? Or you want to change your story before we make a long ride for nothin' and maybe save a couple of lives, includin' your own?'

Gage was staring hard at Trent but the man wouldn't look at him. 'Story's gospel, Tag. I don't have much hope of findin' the satchel, but I've told you what I know about it. One thing, though. . . .'

'No!' snapped Benedict, eyes narrowed. 'No damn deals! You're too damn foxy for my likin', Fargo!'

'Leave Gage behind,' Trent said, ignoring Tag.

Benedict frowned. 'He'll make it.'

'He won't, no sense in it, Tag. He's a greenhorn and he knows nothin' but fireworks and figures in a book. He's hit and he's sufferin'. Leave him be and you won't have any trouble with me.'

Tag snorted, touching his gun. 'I don't figure on havin' any trouble with you anyways!'

'Maybe not. I'd ask that you leave the girl too, but knowin' the way you think. . . .'

'You dunno nothin' about me, even after all the years we've rode together! Now you shut up!'

'Leave Gage behind, Tag.'

'Jesus Christ!' Benedict's eyes were widening now, more white showing around them, giving him a crazy look.'The hell you care about that greenhorn for? He never done you no favours.'

'He did: I owe him, Tag. You don't need him.' Trent flicked his gaze briefly to the woman and away. 'You know you can still control me.'

Tag thought about it, his jaw moving side to side in a

141

characteristic sign that he was considering a problem, teeth making grinding sounds.

'Won't hurt none to take the greenhorn along, I reckon, Tag,' said Chuck Keel and Big Tom nodded, gaze on Trent as if straining to figure just what the man was trying to pull.

'Someone'll get a sawbones and maybe the law out here soon's we go,' he pointed out in his lazy drawl.

'Law ain't nothin' much out here, just a town marshal. Sheriff's over to the County seat. By the time they fetched him we'd be at Horsehead,' Trent pointed out, getting Benedict's attention.

Chuck and Tom sighed: they knew Tag was going to agree to leave Gage behind. Over the years he had often given in to Trent and the only reason they could find was that Fargo had once saved Tag's life in the war, kicked a Yankee bayonet aside an inch from Tag's heart, but Trent had had his leg impaled. Long, long ago but maybe even Tag Benedict could feel obliged to another human being for such a thing.

'All right, Greenhorn stays,' he said suddenly, but shook a finger at Trent. 'We'll have the woman, though. You better take that into account whatever you're stirrin' around in that brain of yours, Fargo!'

Trent looked at her squarely now and nodded briefly. 'I'll remember.'

Her return gaze was cold, mixed with fear.

Gage's was puzzled as Trent knelt beside him and adjusted the bandages Isabella had put in place. 'Try not to get too much weight on that shoulder,' he said quietly, Gage looking straight up into his eyes.

'Why, Fargo?' he whispered hoarsely. 'Why not tell

142

him . . . about . . . Bracemore. . . ?'

'Do that and he'll kill us all just to vent his spleen at missin' out on the diamonds. Need time to figure somethin'. You couldn't make a break for it, but the crew'll get you a doc. Bella can ride so we just might find a chance.'

'Quit that talkin'!' snapped Tag, looking up from his own conference with Chuck and Big Tom. 'Get ready to ride. You, woman, go fetch some grub for us to take along.'

Isabella looked sullen but obeyed. Gage's hand groped for Trent's as he started to rise.

'Take my . . . mount, Fargo . . . He's faster. *Take him!*'

Trent was dragged violently to his feet and Tag hit him on the side of the head, sending him staggering.

'I said get ready, goddamnit! This ain't no picnic! Now mount up and set there till we're ready to go!'

Trent rubbed his head and moved towards Gage's chestnut with its trailing reins. No one said anything when he settled into leather.

He didn't know about it being faster than his own mount, but there was an interesting bulge in the saddlebags.

CHAPTER 12

LOSERS SOMETIMES WIN

Chuck Keel, with his bandaged arm and cut face, couldn't leave Isabella alone as they rode through the hills beyond the last border of the Rosalita spread.

First he rode close and pulled her hair roughly several times, causing her to give small cries of pain and to snatch at the reins as she rocked in the saddle. Trent scowled but Tag laughed and Big Tom gave one of his rare smiles. Chuck Keel challenged Trent with a bleak look, rode in close to the girl again and tried to rip open her blouse.

She slapped him and he grinned coldly, eyes hard and murderous. He hit her across the head and next thing, Trent's horse had rammed into him and unseated him. He rolled out of the saddle as his snorting horse floundered to its feet, right hand streaking for his gun.

Trent rammed his mount into the man again and knocked him flying several feet. Keel rolled in the dust and when he came up to his knees, his Colt was in his hand but he froze when a gun hammer clicked to full cock to his right. He snapped his head that way and saw Benedict covering him.

'Mount up and keep ridin', Chuck.'

'Judas, Tag! You seen what he done! I can't let him get away with that!'

'There'll be time for squarin' away later. Right now I want to get to this Horsehead Pass, find the satchel and be on our way before any Law comes.' The cocked gun was steady on Chuck's chest. 'One less to share with won't make me lose any sleep, Chuck.'

Keel swore softly and put his gun away, but he glared viciously at Trent. 'You'll keep!'

Bella, flushed, shaken, smiled tentatively at Trent but didn't speak. He rode alongside her from there on.

'There is not much hope, I think, Fargo,' she said quietly after a while.

He replied quietly, but honestly. 'Not much, but long as there's some, Bella.'

'I am afraid.'

'I know. If I can, I'll try to hold 'em. You make your run and don't look back or worry about me: if I can work it right, I can handle these fellers.'

'It is very dangerous, Fargo; *they* are very dangerous!'

'Yeah. Me, too. . . .'

They fell quiet as Tag dropped back and rode along on the other side of the girl, flicking his icy stare from Trent to Bella and back again to Trent.

'You want to commit suicide, Fargo, you just try somethin'!'

Trent didn't answer: he was thinking, *But what. . . ?*

They didn't make camp until long after dark and by that time, Trent had figured out where they were. Everyone knew they were headed in the general direction of Horsehead Pass and the prairies but there was a range of hills to cross first.

It came to Trent as they were gathering wood for the campfire: it was the same range where he had stumbled across Clinton Gage, wounded and weak and bleeding to death. Not the exact ridge, but in the same mountains. Which meant they would arrive at the approach to the old pass early tomorrow and then the real trouble would start when Tag knew for certain there were no diamonds.

Trent was sure there would be little signs left of the stampede after all this time and he *knew* there was no satchel of diamonds there, not even the sacks of coins, because ex-sheriff Bracemore had already found them. He felt that Benedict and the others had the notion that all they had to do was scuff the dirt and the satchel and sacks would be exposed. They wouldn't want to dig much but they might make him dig.

There could be a chance then for him to do something, just what he hadn't yet figured. He had to get a good look in those saddlebags on his mount. Gage had *wanted* him to take the chestnut for some other reason than that it would stand the journey better than the horse Trent had ridden into Isabella's. But if he showed any undue interest in the bags, Keel or Tom or Tag himself would be there beside him, looking for themselves.

Then when the fire was going and the girl had been cuffed into preparing a meal, he saw his chance.

Benedict was hungry and kept urging the girl impatiently to get the meal on their plates.

'And I like plenty of spice in my grub,' Tag added sourly.

'I am trying to make do with what we have. In the rush to leave, I forgot the chilli powder and the 'erbs and there are only wild onions for flavour.' She stirred the stew and it smelled OK to Trent but he stood casually and moved to where he had dumped the saddle from the chestnut.

'Gage likes a lot of spice in his grub. He might have some.'

He knelt and fumbled at the straps, Chuck Keel and Big Tom adding their urgings to the girl, Tom talking about the way his sister could cook a jack-rabbit on an open fire, using the wild herbs amd grasses.

Trent was surprised to find a couple of paper bags as he groped around, feeling they were half full of powder, he guessed. Maybe flour, or salt, or. . . .

'The hell you think you're doin'!' Tag roared suddenly jumping to his feet.

Trent looked casually over his shoulder although his heart was hammering. He closed that bag and started on the second. 'Tryin' to find some spices but, oh-oh!, what's this?'

It was a small jar of paprika, less then half full, but it saved the day. Trent tossed it towards the advancing Benedict who caught it instinctively, dropping his hand from his gun-butt as he did so. He looked at the torn and faded label and grinned, going back to where

Isabella crouched by the small fire.

He unscrewed the cap and up-ended the jar into the stew.

'Too much!' she protested, turning her head to sneeze.

'Just right, now hurry it along!'

When they ate, there was far too much paprika in the stew and they all drank deeply from the water bottles and the coffee pot had to be brewed up three times before their raw throats felt any ease.

'Muh belly's on fire,' said Big Tom, burping noisily. 'But it sure was a good stoo!'

Chuck said it was too hot for him but Tag allowed it was OK. 'Needed a touch of chilli and some sage, though. All right. Git the mess cleared away and we'll turn in. Early start tomorrow.' He smiled crookedly at Trent. 'Could be a good day or a bad one all round, eh, Fargo?'

'In the lap of the gods, Tag,' Trent allowed and started to help the girl, scraping the plates into the fire that was burning down now.

'Hurry it up,' Benedict growled. 'I'm tired and I aim to see you trussed like a turkey before I turn in, Fargo.'

Trent didn't react: he had fully expected this and was preparing himself for a night-long struggle with his bonds. The girl, too, he knew, would be tied up and he was worried about it: with her helpless, Keel might try something again. He was pretty sure Benedict wouldn't interfere this time.

They were dumped not far apart in the shadow of a low overhang where they were cramped and unable to move about much. Trent was watching Keel closely but the man was more concerned with his cut arm now and the pain it was giving him. He nagged Big Tom into undoing the bandage and looking at the cut that had been made by the girl's knife.

'Can't see none too good in this light, but it sure looks mighty red to me, streaks goin' into your armpit. An' it's swelled up, too.'

Chuck sucked down a sharp breath. 'Well, woman! What do I do about it? You're the goddamn nurse!'

'I left all the medicines with Mr Gage,' she replied sleepily. 'If it hurts, wash it with warm water with salt dissolved in it.'

'Aaah. You bitch! I oughta. . . .'

'Shut up!' Tag growled, settling into his bedroll. 'Just do it or bandage it up again or somethin', but let me sleep!'

Keel swore and got into more trouble, clattering the pans and bowls about while hunting for the salt. But he finally finished bathing the wound and announced it did feel a lot better. Big Tom was not pleased when he was prodded awake by Chuck to help replace the bandage.

Finally, the camp was quiet except for the infrequent crackling of the dying fire. Keel heaved and tossed for a long time under his blanket before he finally fell asleep, snoring with the others.

Trent was still awake although he had faked sleep, and now he tried to stretch his bonds enough so as to slip a hand free. It took only minutes for him to realize he wasn't going to do it: the ropes were too tight and he was already losing feeling in his hands and fingers. Skin was rubbed off and his flesh stung. He swore, louder than he meant to apparently, for the girl rolled over close to him, her body pressing against his.

'You saw me drive the *cuchillo* into the porch post,' she whispered, her breath warm against his ear. 'I have another, as Benedict said, strapped to my thigh.'

Trent thought it was as well Keel hadn't started fondling her, but, 'How do we get to it?'

He felt her lips draw back in a smile. 'You will have to work your hands under my skirt and ease it out of the sheath.' She smothered a small laugh as he stiffened and knew he was embarrassed. 'Don't be shy, Fargo! Our very lives may depend on this!'

He swallowed and she moved around carefully and he felt the hem of her skirts. He had to hitch and roll to get his hands up her leg to the thigh, his weight pinning her left leg now. She sucked down a sharp breath as stones bit into her. His fingers, numbing with the tightness of the ropes, fumbled at the soft leather and he felt himself flush, the sweat start as he touched the edge of her panties.

The hell with this! he thought savagely. *She's right: our lives depend on it! So. . . .*

So he groped and tugged and pried and finally got the short-bladed *cuchillo* free of the soft leather. He managed to hold it even though he had little feeling in his hands now, wormed away from her. The blade caught the material of her skirt and he heard it rip a little before it came free. He dropped it and groped frantically to find it again.

By then she had worked her body around and her slim fingers felt along his rigid wrists to the knife and she took it from him. Her bonds were not as tight as his and she had almost full feeling in her hands and was able to grip the knife firmly. He moved his wrists around and by mutual co-operation and the loss of a little flesh and some blood, she got the blade in between his wrists. Then he began to work his arms up and down, feeling the burning needles of pain in his shoulders because of the awkward position, the bonds making contact with the razor-edged blade.

Fibres popped one by one and he got too enthusiastic at one stage and the steel dug into his flesh, bringing an oath and an involuntary grunt of pain. He froze as Tag Benedict heaved over in his bedroll, murmuring. Big Tom continued his rafter-shaking snore and Chuck Keel coughed, muttered something, and turned over, tugging his single blanket firmly about his shoulders.

Breathing hard, Trent gave them a few minutes to settle, went to work on the bonds again and in seconds the last strand parted and his hands flew apart with the tension he had had on them and the knife clattered on the gravel. Both went rigid, holding their breath, but the three outlaws didn't stir.

Rubbing his hands to get feeling in them, the flesh slippery with blood, Trent found the knife, sliced his ankle ropes and then cut the girl free. He could just make out her features in the glow of the fire, which was mainly coals now. The red reflected in her dark eyes and from her hair. He saw her smile and he nodded, squeezed her hand.

'I need the knife a little longer,' he said and she grabbed his hand as he reached for it.

'You aren't going to. . . .'

He shook his head. 'I ought to slit their throats but,

no, I've a better idea. Can you ride bareback?'

'I have but I don't like it.'

'You'll have to get used to it. Start creeping towards the horses, *now!*'

She turned and obeyed as he squatted and crab-walked silently to the saddlebags. He brought out the two small paper bags, slit the sides and lifted one to sniff cautiously. He smiled in the night: just as he had hoped.

The girl was at the horses now and she had two mounts, leading them by the reins: *Good! He hadn't even had to tell her to put the bridles on.*

He took the packets and ripped the slits open a little more as he approached the coals of the fire. He saw Benedict's rifle on the ground beside his bedroll. Big Tom had his rifle close to hand too, but it looked like Chuck Keel was sleeping with his sixgun in his hand under the blankets.

Waving an arm in the direction of the up slope, Trent watched the girl lead the horses that way, stiffened when one knocked two stones together with a loud *clunk!* Tag started to stir and this time he was waking up.

Trent yelled to Bella, 'Go! Get goin' now!'

That was all it took to throw the camp into chaos as she started to run up the slope leading the horses. Tag started up and Trent kicked him savagely, knocking him sprawling as he lunged for the fire, tipping both packets of gunpowder onto the coals.

The powder almost smothered the coals for an instant and then it exploded, not an ear-shattering, destructive explosion because it was unconfined, but the gunpowder ignited so fast that there was a rushing *whoosh!* and choking smoke writhed and swirled in roiling clouds with a suddenness that caught Trent himself in the midst of it.

His breath was cut off, his face was seared and he was blinded as the thick, heavy smoke burst over him like surf at the sea's edge. It filled the camp, obliterating it in impenetrable fog. Men were yelling, coughing, choking, cursing. A gun crashed and he made out the blurred stab of flame pointing away from him.

'Watch it, goddamnit!' roared Tag Benedict. 'Watch where you're shootin'!'

Trent groped towards the sound but Keel's voice spoke only a foot from him.

'The hell's happened? I can't see!' He began to cough and then Trent struck out blindly. His fist thudded into a body and Keel grunted and Trent followed through, one hand punching, the other trying to get a grip on the man's clothing.

His fingers twisted in coarse cloth and he hauled in sharply and crashed his head forward. He heard nose cartilage crush and felt the warm spray of blood as Keel choked back a cry of agony. A sixgun blasted almost in his face and then he had the hand in his grip, wrenched and twisted, Keel shouting as his finger caught up in the trigger-guard and snapped. Trent reversed the gun and thrust it forward, firing the instant the barrel touched the man's body. Keel was blown backwards and then Trent found himself at the edge of the smoke screen, stepped clear, coughing.

A big blurred shape came after him and he saw it was Big Tom, bringing up the rifle. Trent dropped to one knee, triggered upwards twice. Big Tom Santos stopped in his tracks as the lead angled up through his barrel chest. His thick legs started to sag but he bared his teeth and with a roar like a lion, straightened and swung the rifle around.

Trent's gun hammer fell on an empty chamber.

He dived for the ground as Tom's rifle whiplashed and he rolled behind the big man, kicked him in the back of the legs. Santos grunted and started to stumble. Trent bounced to his feet, swung a wild punch that almost broke his hand as it skimmed off Big Tom's hard head, and he wrenched the rifle from the man's grip. Tom was already falling when Trent shot him again. The body twisted and hit the ground with an audible thump.

Instinct and knife-edge reflexes made Trent spin away and dive flat. Through the roiling smoke that was gradually clearing, he saw four daggers of flame, moving slightly in a short arc, as Tag Benedict triggered and levered, hoping the spread of shot would find Fargo Trent.

But the bullets did no more than rip through the shroud of smoke. Trent rolled onto his belly, levering a shell into the rifle's breech, fired just above those stabbing muzzle flashes. He heard Tag go down but there were other sounds too, and he knew the man wasn't fatally hit.

The smoke rolled away and he blinked his burning, running eyes fast in an effort to clear his vision. He could just make out the blur of Tag's body as the man rolled over and over across the clearing, thrust up to his knees, rifle braced into his hip.

Trent was ready, his own rifle braced firmly in the

same manner, and he worked trigger and lever in a brief blurring speed that punched three bullets into Tag, throwing the man's body into macabre contortions. His rifle fell but Tag was dead before it hit the ground.

'Fargo?' Bella's voice called tentatively, fearfully into the sudden silence as the echoes died away and the smoke gradually lifted.

'Here,' he said quietly and she came to him in a rush, throwing her arms about him, trying to crush him in her eagerness to feel for herself that he was indeed safe.

Sheriff Andy Quinnell was waiting when they reached the ranch.

Gage was sitting on the porch in a cane chair while the sheriff sat on the rail smoking, watching with pinched-down eyes as the small cavalcade approached. Trent and the girl rode side by side but Trent was holding the reins of the first of three horses trailing behind with a dead man roped across each.

Quinnell flicked the cigarette away quickly as he stood, a hand on his gun-butt. 'Trent, by God!' he hissed.

Gage, arm in a sling, said, 'Easy, sheriff. I think he's brought you a gift.'

Quinnell frowned and glanced sharply at Gage. 'The hell you talkin' about? He's bringin' in three dead men!'

'Each one worth at least a thousand dollars. And if, as I believe, that's Tag Benedict on the lead horse, I reckon he ought to be worth as much as *five* thousand.'

'To Trent? He's a wanted man himself. He can't

claim no bounty.'

'No, but maybe you could, unless Trent said *you* had nothing to do with apprehending the outlaws and he'd have a fine woman of high regard in Isabella to back him.'

The sheriff glanced back at the cavalcade that had now entered the yard. Isabella and Fargo Trent were dismounting stiffly. Both were begrimed and when closer smelled distinctly of gunpowder.

Trent nodded to Quinnell and introduced Isabella. 'I'm pleased you are here, sheriff. We were abducted by these three outlaws, but, fortunately, Mr Trent subdued them as you see.'

'I was just telling Sheriff Quinnell, Fargo, how it's kind of uncertain who is going to be able to collect the bounty on these men,' Gage said with a meaningful look at Quinnell.

The sheriff's pistol came up suddenly, covering Trent. 'I can claim it on *him!* He's now my prisoner.'

'Sheriff! This man saved my life and . . .' began Isabella but Gage cut in calmly.

'I was also telling the sheriff that while the bounty couldn't be paid to Fargo or himself, seeing as he had nothing to do with the capture and killing of the Benedict gang, that it's possible some . . . arrangement could be made.'

Trent flicked his eyes to Gage. 'What kind of arrangement?'

'Well, Sheriff Quinnell seems intent on arresting you so he can claim the thousand dollar bounty on your head. I was about to suggest just as you arrived, that you might be induced to hand over the three dead outlaws to him and, er, allow him to claim capture and there-fore bounty as well.'

Trent was silent for a few moments. The girl seemed to be holding her breath. Quinnell remained deadpan.

'Why would I do that, Gage?' Trent asked quietly.

'In exchange for your freedom. I've been telling Andy here how hard you've been trying to get onto the straight and narrow, that you really want to leave the owlhoot trail behind.'

'They never leave it far behind!' Quinnell growled, but somehow it sounded like something he felt he had to say, rather than a firm conviction.

'If a man's given a decent chance,' Gage said, 'by some understanding lawman, perhaps, and he has a good woman to back him, well, one less outlaw on the loose seems a fair trade to me.'

'And you figure I can be bribed, huh?' Andy Quinnell said curtly. 'Not only bribed, but live a lie about how I gunned down these three outlaws in a shoot-out. . . .' His voice trailed off and they saw it in his face: *he liked the idea!*

Whether it was true or not, he saw he could be an overnight hero, a *rich* overnight hero because he would resign from the law office so there could be no conflict of interest in his claim for the bounties. Folk would look up to him. He could write his story or have it writ-ten by one of these dime novelists for a fee. He could be *famous* after a lifetime of obscurity. He coughed to clear his throat.

'It would be more like a reward than a . . . bribe, Andy,' Gage pointed out quietly and that swung it all the way.

'Suppose we made that deal, I dunno as I'd care for you bein' within spittin' distance of my town, Trent! you might get ideas sometime an'. . . .'

'You wouldn't have to stay in Drumhead, Andy,' Gage said persuasively. 'After the first big welcome and celebration you could go just about anywhere you liked! You'll be rich and famous.'

Quinnell was kind of slow but finally he caught on. He set his hard eyes on Trent. 'Deal?'

'I'm happy with it.'

'Where you gonna be? Here?'

Trent looked at Bella and she smiled.

That was answer enough.

'Gage,' Trent said, holding Bella's hand, 'I think you just became a fully-fledged Westerner.'

Gage flapped a casual hand, smiling. 'Well, mostly all you have to do is learn to think deviously.' He winked at Isabella and added to Trent, 'And I had a good teacher.'

Trent sighed. 'I see I'm gonna have to complete your education: show you how to use a gun properly.'

Gage frowned, puzzled.

'Talkin' like that, you could get yourself shot.'

Gage looked so shocked that Trent and Isabella couldn't keep from chuckling.

Even Andy Quinnell smiled.